Caution in the Wind

Book One: Partnerships

a novel

by

William N. Gilmore

William N. Gilmore

First Printing

Book design by William N. Gilmore
Cover art by Heather Trim of TrimVentures Media
www.TrimVentures.com

This is a work of fiction. Any references to historical events,
real people, or real locals are used fictitiously. Other
characters, settings, places, or events are entirely of the
author's imagination. Any resemblance to actual events, locals,
or persons, living or dead is entirely coincidental.

ISBN:978-1-946689-03-0
Manufactured by CreateSpace ©
www.createspace.com

Printed in the United States of America

Caution in the Wind

Book One: Partnerships

To Gina, Enjoy the adventure. William N. Gilmore APD

William N. Gilmore

Books

by

William N. Gilmore

Books in the Larry Gillam and Sam Lovett

Detective Series

Book One:

BLUE BLOODS & BLACK HEARTS

Book Two:

GOLD BADGES & DARK SOULS

Book Three:

BLUE KNIGHTS & WHITE LIES

Other Books:

Saints, Sinners, Lovers and Others

Poems and Prose

From Thoughts That Arose

Remembering Mike

Acknowledgements

First and always, I want to thank my wife, Esther, for her help, support, guidance, love, insight, knowledge, and patience. Without her, this would be a disaster from the beginning.

Our entire family. Love you guys.

The Paulding County Writers Guild, especially its founder, the late Dana Freeman; Author Deanna Oaks and her infamous red pen; Author Bryan Powell, owner of the Hiram Bookstore; Alex, his youth, talent, and dedication inspires us all; and all the other members who have been so helpful.

Retired Atlanta Police Detective Mary Pealor, friend, supporter, fan, editor, hot chick, and a real bad ass. Thank you, so very much. This one's on me.

All my police buddies. Extraordinary heroes, every day!

All my army buddies. Thank you, for your service.

All my metal detecting buddies. Finders of lost history.

All my poker buddies (who buy my books anyway).

All my Republican buddies. MAGA.

All my Democrat buddies. All three (oops, one finally converted) all two of you.

And anyone else I did not mention.

Secret deals between governments are normal. Secret deals between governments and individuals are rare. Secret deals between governments and individuals who want to disrupt the political agendas of their government are not spoken of and official records are not kept.

William N. Gilmore

Prologue

Joseph Long, a member of the soon to be established American and Foreign Anti-Slavery Society just finished sealing a secret deal with government agents of England in the early months of 1840.

He traveled far and at great peril to do so, assuming a false name with supporting documents which would pass almost any scrutiny. He had volunteered for this dangerous assignment.

Few knew of his true mission or the consequences if he were to fail. He was an abolitionist from the South, supported by the North, and seeking financial assistance from a foreign country; to some, he might be considered a threat, to many, a hero, and then to others, a traitor.

The American anti-slavery movement needed funds to support their political cause, and England, although reluctant in the past to provide support, was now ready to back them; at least, to a point and with complete anonymity.

England had its own successful anti-slavery movement and with the 1833 Act of Parliament of the United Kingdom, The Slavery Abolition Act, slavery was abolished throughout the British Empire. The exceptions were for Territories in the possession of the East India Company.

Violence over the slavery issue was spreading, especially in New York, and whispers of secession were now in the air.

An unwanted yet determined civil action spread its early roots in the minds of more than a few.

Slavery was a blight on the nation, yet it also helped to sustain the nation. With the South's agricultural economy supplying the industrial North with cotton and tobacco, among other items, the North, for the most part, turned a blind eye to the situation while at the same time, calling slavery a great evil.

The abolitionist movement progressed for years before splintering into several factions to obtain their objectives, each in their own way; at least one group by political means and others by much more aggressive tactics.

With the secret pact Long made with England, the Royal Treasury was relieved of all the gold sovereigns and half sovereigns minted for that year; none of the coins were ever placed into circulation, along with the gold bullion set aside for their continued mintage. Nearly a million dollars in British gold was going to support the anti-slavery movement in the United States.

All records of the pact were ordered destroyed and those involved were sworn to secrecy or threatened so as not to have any evidence of England's direct participation.

A special ship, one that carried many different flags along with a hand-picked crew was provided. The British gold would soon be on its way to the shores of the United States. It would be melted down and re-struck in an attempt to keep the young country united and wipe the stain of slavery from its land by financially backing the new Liberty Party.

However, unforeseen circumstances, bad luck, or whatever you wish to call it, raised its ugly head and Long never reached the United States. The ship with its secret cargo of gold disappeared right along with him, becoming a legend and thus, sealing the fate of many thousands of slaves for decades, or even longer, and possibly even the soul of the great nation.

William N. Gilmore

CHAPTER 1

The man was showing the young boy, his grandson, how to use the metal detector he bought him for his tenth birthday. It wasn't a toy, but it also wasn't one of the really expensive, high-end models either. On the second day of their family beach vacation and as planned, they snuck out early before anyone else awoke.

The sun, just peeking over the watery horizon, gave some of the multi-red hued clouds a widening rustic stain. The low tide's waves came rushing in, trying desperately to catch the receding waters which just washed the gently sloping sand before it. Seagulls and sandpipers ran back and forth trying to catch a meal.

The grandfather tossed a few coins out on the dry beach for the boy to see how the detector reacted to them. The boy's eyes grew wide. He was thrilled to hear the beeping in the headphones as he waved the coil over one of the areas where a coin landed, burying itself from sight.

"I think I found one, Grandpa Bill!" the boy exclaimed.

"That's great, Sam. Now dig it out like I showed you."

Using the square, yellow-plastic scoop with small holes all through it to let the sand out, but not so big as to let coins escape, the boy dipped it into the dry, white sand taking a good helping. He shook the scoop until all the sand filtered through the holes, leaving a trapped coin rattling.

"It's a dime, Grandpa!"

"Good job. Now see if you can find some more."

After just a few minutes, the boy called out again, "I got another one. It's a quarter," he declared with a large grin.

"That's really good. I didn't throw out a quarter. You found that one on your own."

"We're going to be rich in no time," the boy beamed. "I'm going to find some pirate treasure."

"I wouldn't be surprised," the man laughed, hoping his grandson would find at least a dollar or two of lost change before they needed to head in. He made his way closer to the surf, looking for any interesting seashells or shark's teeth as he kept his other eye on Sam. The boy was genuinely enjoying himself and followed the instructions he was given.

Having found a number of coins along the sandy beach, Sam ventured closer to the water himself, sometimes digging the scoop into the wet sand and washing it away by dipping it into the water as he was taught, hoping to find a coin left behind in the scoop.

More times than not, it was a bobby pin, some foil, or

some other small, indistinguishable, metallic item mixed in with an assortment of small, colorful shells. After about twenty minutes, Sam ran up to his grandfather, talking a mile a minute and a little too loudly due to the headphones over his ears.

"I think I found some pirate treasure, Grandpa. It was deep in the wet sand. It's really pretty and I think it's gold."

"Alright, let's see this wonderful treasure," Grandpa Bill laughed, expecting to see maybe another coin, or maybe just a pretty golden colored, round seashell.

"It's got a woman on it and some strange writing," Sam continued, as he held out his closed hand.

Grandpa Bill held out his hand under Sam's. Now he was thinking it could be a foreign coin or it could even be one of those gold-colored, aluminum condom tins. That would be a little hard for him to explain to a ten-year-old.

Sam dropped the object into his grandpa's open hand. It had some weight to it and it was the shape and size of a medium coin; slightly larger than a nickel, but not as thick. Grandpa Bill took a closer look at the object with his old eyes, not having brought his glasses out with him. Even without them, he could tell this was something special.

The coin had a gold tone to it with the slightly worn image of a woman on one side and what looked like a crown over a coat of arms on the other. He wiped off some of the crusty sand and could just make out some of the letters as he tromboned his arm back and forth. It looked like the thing might be British.

Squinting at the numbers below the woman's profile, he thought he read a date of eighteen hundred something.

"Are you kidding me?" he said out loud. He was now scared to rub the coin any more than he or Sam had already done.

"It is pirate treasure, isn't it, Grandpa?" Sam asked.

"I'm not sure what it is. We'll have to get it checked out, maybe by a coin dealer. I'll hold on to it, for now, we don't want you to lose it."

"I bet it's worth a million bucks. I'm going to find some more. There might be a whole treasure chest there," Sam speculated, running back to the site of his find.

Grandpa Bill continued to look at the coin. "It's possible," he said to the wind and surf, "it's just possible."

The week after returning home from their vacation, Grandpa Bill picked up Sam from his daughter's house just outside Atlanta and went to one of the downtown coin dealers to have the coin identified.

The dealer, Tom Dearing, the new owner of Quality Coins and Stamps, hearing the delightful story from Sam himself, was happy to help. Disappointedly, Sam told him no other "pirate treasure" was found.

The dealer looked at the coin under a magnifying glass, gave a funny look and then got another, more powerful jeweler's loop.

"What beach did you say you found this?" The dealer asked as he put the coin on a small electronic scale.

"We didn't say," Grandpa Bill answered before Sam could speak up. "Let's just say we found it on the East Coast."

"It's real gold, isn't it? It came from a pirate, didn't it?" The young boy asked, not able to hold back his excitement any longer.

"It appears to be a gold British Sovereign," the dealer said, not looking up from the coin. "It has a young Queen Victoria on one side and the British shield and crown on the other. It's dated 1840. I'd say it's been in the water for most of its life. I can't say it came from a pirate, but it's pretty old. Maybe it did. Let me look in one of my books for some more information."

The dealer turned and took a book from a shelf behind him. He flipped several pages and seemed to be reading. He raised his head and looked at Grandpa Bill for a few seconds and went back to reading. He turned and took another book down and searched for something in that book. He went back to the first book and then took a longer look at the coin, flipping it over, examining the edge, measuring it, and once again, he put it on the scale.

Finally, the dealer gave his opinion. "I believe what you have is a counterfeit or a fantasy coin. My research shows the Brit's never minted a sovereign like this in 1840. It doesn't exist, not officially. It could be a movie prop or just a trinket someone made. The only real value would be the gold itself."

"I don't think a movie prop would be made of real gold," Grandpa Bill stated, "and I wouldn't call this a trinket."

"I can offer you a couple hundred dollars for it," the dealer said. "That would buy you a mighty nice bicycle, young man," he hinted, trying to tempt Sam.

"I think we'll hold onto it for a while," Grandpa Bill proclaimed. Sam's shoulders slumped a bit. "Something the grandson can show off for a while."

"I might lose a little, but I could go as high as five-hundred. It would be a good start on the kid's college fund," now working on Grandpa Bill.

"We'll think it over," Grandpa Bill stated, holding out his hand to receive the coin back.

"Here, let me put it in a protective cover for you," The dealer offered. "No charge."

"Thank you," Grandpa Bill said, receiving the coin back now in a small, clear, plastic case which he dropped into his shirt pocket. And thanks for your time and the information."

As soon as Grandpa Bill and Sam left the store, the coin dealer wrote down the license plate of their car as it drove away then quickly hurried to the phone.

CHAPTER 2

The sweet voice of a child followed by her high-pitched laughter came from behind the closed door of the room. Her mother, walking along the upstairs hallway, stopped and lightly tapped on the bedroom door.

"Caution, what are you doing, sweetheart?" she asked as she opened the door just a crack.

"Nothing, Mother, just playing."

"Who are you talking to, dear?"

"No one, Mother. I'm just playing with my dolls."

"Okay dear, you can stay in your room for now, but don't be running or be too loud. Your father is having one of his business meetings in the study."

"Sorry, Mother. We'll be quieter."

Caution's mother gave a little laugh herself as she closed the door. Her daughter possessed a vivid imagination believing the dolls could be too loud as well.

Caution was still only nine years old and although there were times she wanted to spend with her parents, it seemed she preferred spending more and more time alone in her room playing rather than helping around the house, or even going outside when there were no visitors, or when the weather was beautiful. Her mother didn't believe there was any real reason for concern, at least, not yet.

Caution was a sweet surprise after several failed attempts at having a family; coming very late in her parent's lives. Other couples of their age already had children and most of those were now grown.

There were no other children close to her age nearby and she was an only child. The few friends she did have attended her private school but were not close. Yet, it had not been an unhappy or lonely childhood for Caution. She was extremely devoted to her parents and she always found things to keep herself occupied.

There were numerous housekeepers and governesses hired to help with Caution and to assist with the large house. Some were attentive to Caution, but most didn't stay for long. Some didn't even last more than a few days or give any notice before they were gone.

After a while, Caution's mother stopped relying on anyone else and chose to give up her career to stay home and attend to her daughter's needs herself. After all, she didn't need to work. The family was considerably well off from inheritances, good investments, and business holdings.

There was even a large office complex bearing the family name near the downtown area along with the new construction of a forty-story office building, complete with underground parking and a penthouse.

Her mother knew that at some point Caution would grow out of the dolls and her imaginary friends, but for now, she let her have her childhood. There were too many worries in this world grown-ups faced every day. She and Caution's father were all too aware of that sad fact.

"Shhh. I told you she would hear us," Caution warned as she poured the invisible tea from a miniature porcelain kettle into the tiny, flowered cup.

"It wasn't me. It was you who was making all the noise. She can't hear me, remember?"

"But why not, Grandpa?" she asked, setting the small cup and saucer in front of him as they sat cross-legged on the blanket under the window. "Why won't you let them hear you and see you like I do?"

"As I've told you before, darling, I don't think it's me. I believe it's because they don't know they can. They become too busy with themselves and are looking too much inside instead of all around. It's something that happens to people when they grow up."

"But you scared off the ladies who came to work here. How did you do that?"

"Although there were a few who seemed nice, they can't love and take care of you like your own family can," he said, with a ghostly smile. "Some of them didn't really care about

21

your wellbeing. Some had questionable pasts or dark hearts, and some were just thick in the head. The few things I was able to do were enough to give them reasons not to want to stay."

"I think they would like to see you, especially Father," Caution said. "Sometimes I see him looking at your picture and reading your letters. He doesn't talk about you much, but I still think he would have loved to have known you in person."

"As would I, but just as promised, you must never tell them about me. Do you understand?"

"Not really, Grandpa, but if you say so. It will be our secret. I wish you could stay forever. Where do you go when you leave?" Caution asked.

Standing and beginning a slow pace, he brought one arm up across his chest, cupping the elbow of the other, and setting his chin between the thumb and forefinger of his mostly closed hand. Deep in thought, her great-great-grandfather spoke as he stared at the floor. "It's hard to say. I'm not really sure. It's not like there is a time or place for me to be somewhere and there are times when all I want is to be with you, but alas, I can't."

"Are you in Heaven, Grandpa?"

He looked down at her and smiled. "I'm not sure, sweetheart. I think I am or at least, I think I'm on my way. Maybe I'm just on a waiting list and have to stay close by for a bit. I know I'm not in the other place. Not if I'm able to visit with you."

"That's good," Caution said, with a giggle. "And you know what Grandpa?"

"What would that be, my darling?"

"I hope I never grow up as long as you're around."

"Wouldn't that be nice?" Grandpa Patrick said.

Caution was always a happy child. Even as a baby, she would be quick to giggle and coo instead of cry. Her alert, bright green eyes always seemed focused on a distant object while an enduring smile played on her face. Her long, blazing red hair came from her father's side of the family. She was a third generation American of Irish descent. Something of which she would always be proud.

William N. Gilmore

CHAPTER 3

Young Patrick Murphy, Caution's great-great-grandfather, was the son of a weaver and the first of the family to leave the Emerald Isle and come to America. Thousands of other people from all over the world came to these shores to escape their heartaches and to start a new life. Many escaping disease and famine, some seeking the fruitful land, or their fortunes in the recently discovered gold fields of California. The sad reality was few of those adventurers saw those dreams come to pass.

Ireland was going through another potato famine. The 1848 famine was not as bad as the 1846 potato famine, but it still caused many problems. The truth was that Ireland had plenty of food. In fact, it exported many shiploads to other countries. It was the price of food. The poor could not afford to buy food enough to sustain themselves.

Many diseases came about because of poor nutrition: cholera, typhoid, dysentery, and tuberculosis, just to name a few. A whole generation attempted to flee. Ships were crowded, exposing all to the raging microbes.

The six-week passage across the inhospitable Atlantic Ocean took its toll. Sometimes, on what came to be known as 'coffin ships'; one in five travelers never survived the journey.

Families were ripped apart, some wiped out. The risk was high. Maybe no worse than staying in Ireland, where starvation and disease were rampant, potato farms failing, and unrest abounded.

As an intelligent and determined young man, Patrick left his uncle's home where he lived since his parent's death a few years earlier, victims of 'famine disease', as it came to be called.

He was set on making his own escape and finding his place in the world. However, things did not go as smoothly as he hoped. He soon found himself without means and not wanting to return to his uncle, he resorted to odd jobs in the city, sleeping in the backs of the stores or in the horse stables he cleaned.

While sweeping one of the shops, he noticed a shiny object on the floor. He reached down, picked it up and turned it in his fingers. He was mesmerized by its elegant beauty. It was a silver embossed thimble.

"Are you trying to steal from me, lad?" Came a thunderous voice.

"No sir, of course not. I—I just found this on the floor as I was sweeping, sir. I was just looking at it. It's beautiful."

"Hand it to me," the shopkeeper demanded.

Patrick did as he was told, holding out the thimble in his outstretched hand.

The man looked down at the thimble in Patrick's hand for a few seconds. It was easy to see the young man's hand, calloused and cracked, was of someone who worked hard, but he also noticed Patrick's hand was not shaking as a scared thief's who had just been caught. Furthermore, Patrick looked him in the eyes when he spoke to him.

"I have been looking for that thimble for a while," the shopkeeper said, with a huff, and quickly snatched it from Patrick's hand. "Now, get back to work."

In time, Patrick became the apprentice to the widowed, wealthy, and rather portly tailor who had no children to pass along his trade. Although apprentice was too grand a word for what Patrick really did: cleaning and sweeping, shining the tailor's boots, cooking meals when necessary, and running errands.

The tailor was not the kindest of people for whom to work. He was impatient and quick-tempered, and his large, shiny boots often landed a mighty kick on Patrick's backside. He may even have his reasons for being bitter and taking out his frustrations on the young lad, but the position provided Patrick with a warm place to sleep and food to eat. Things could have been, and had been, much worse.

Eventually, when things did turn worse, the tailor fled the country in the wake of the looming economic downfall. Patrick, without any other resources, found himself with little other choice, but to follow.

By now, Patrick was obliged by a contract to the tailor to

work for a period of time as compensation for his passage and for his day to day expenses. The contract was the only way Patrick would have been able to make it to America. He knew it was set up so he would never be able to make enough money to pay off his continuing debt.

Although the term commonly used was 'indentured servant', he knew he would be little better than a slave, but he continued to have hope; and fate, like a shadow on a bright day, dogged his every step.

The ship on which they were to make their escape was not a regular passenger ship; it was not registered, and there was not a posted schedule; tickets were not sold, and a passenger list was not kept. You only found out about the sailing by word of mouth or were referred by someone for a price.

Questions, on either side, were not asked. The captain was obviously not the most reputable man and, as such, would not sail into a big port, but would have to arrive in darkness at a clandestine location.

He took on only those who could pay the heavy fees up front. The ship's cargo was loaded under heavily armed guard and everyone was turned away until it was completely hauled aboard and stored.

Bribes and special fees were paid to slip out of port without the proper papers or inspections. Comfort was not on the menu. The crew wanted nothing to do with you unless robbery, or worse, was on their mind. Portions of the ship were off limit's the entire trip and guards were ready to cut your throat if you came too close.

Nearing the end of the long voyage, the new shores of America appeared on the horizon, but the waters were not calm that last day and they began churning much more heavily. A ferocious storm rose suddenly as they oft times do at sea.

As the moonless curtain of night fell, the ship's crew was unable to maneuver her to the safety of a port or into deeper, calmer waters before a terrible gale took complete control of her, pushing her towards the shore. The storm's mighty waves angrily smashed her against hidden rocky breakers, time and time again. The main mast broke, falling on several of the terrified crew, killing them instantly.

As they took on water, Patrick knew they couldn't stay down in the ship any longer. The tailor, who fought seasickness most of the voyage, refused to leave his cabin, even at the insistence of his young protégé. There was no way to get him to leave and his large bulk prevented him from being carried out.

Patrick refused to stay any longer and he and a lucky few clambered to the top deck. One of the other fortunate persons making it to the top was a fellow Irishman named Michael Shannon Andrew O'Brien. They became friends on the voyage, although Michael, or Big Mike as Patrick liked to call him, was several years older and towered over Patrick.

Michael, as he told anyone who would listen, was on his way to California to strike it big in gold, and one day soon he would build himself a castle on a hill overlooking the Pacific Ocean.

Somehow having found each other on the deck of the rolling ship, Patrick knew they would have to go into the raging water and swim for their lives before the ship took them down with it.

"Michael!" Patrick yelled, praying he might be heard over the squall. "We have to get off the ship. We'll die here if we don't."

As the ship bucked and turned, they maneuvered their way to the rail.

"Jump when I say," Patrick yelled.

"I can't," Michael shouted, shaking his head vigorously while trying to hold onto the slick rail.

The ship was quickly breaking apart, but Michael could not be made to jump, even after Patrick told him again they would surely die on the ship if they stayed.

"Yes, you can. You have to," Patrick insisted.

"No," Michael was quick to return, violently shaking his head.

Patrick knew they couldn't wait any longer and at the last moment, forced Michael's grip loose from the slippery rail and pushed his new friend into the sinister, dark sea, following right behind. Patrick found out almost too late that Michael couldn't swim a lick.

Once in the water, his bulk, along with those big arms flaying all around, made him something impossible, or at least, something less than desirable, to hold onto during the raging storm. He surely would have pulled anyone under the water trying to keep himself afloat whether he meant to or not.

Patrick, through some mighty determination and even more, luck, was able to get to his friend and get him tied to a large broken, yet floating piece of the ship's mast and rigging before the powerful waves separated them.

Several made it safely to the shore; others with them were barely conscious, broken and bloody, some cut to the bone by the sharp barnacles and jagged rocks, while many others made the nearly three-thousand-mile journey only to perish within the last several hundred yards of the new land.

Miraculously, the doomed ship was spotted by a coastal watch and an alarm went out. Patrick found himself being helped out of the foamy surf by several men responding from a nearby village. A dry, warm blanket was placed over his shoulders and he was being helped away from the churning water.

After just a few steps, he thought he heard a voice on the wind.

"Help! Help me!" Barely audible within the raging storm. Patrick turned, throwing off the blanket and leaving his escort, he ran back to the surf. He stopped, cupped his ears, straining to listen; the wind, the waves, nothing more.

The men who plucked Patrick from the water were trying to pull him away once again. A powerful bolt of lightning streaked across the sky, illuminating everything for a moment as Patrick scanned the water. Among all the floating debris, he saw him at the top of a swell, one arm raised, not more than twenty meters from shore, still tied to the broken section of the mast.

"Bloody hell, Mike! I'm coming!" Patrick screamed into the storm.

Once again, he abandoned his rescuers. Rushing into the dangerous waves, fighting the incoming wall of water to get to his friend. His arms already over-labored, he swam like a madman for what seemed like forever to get to where Mike's head was barely above the water.

"I'm here, Mike. I'm here." There was no movement or sound now from the limp form.

Patrick grabbed onto the rope still restraining Mike to the scarcely buoyant timber, fighting with the wet knots to release the hold. Freeing Mike from the mast, Patrick bit down hard on the trailing rope still wrapped around Mike to use both hands and arms for the grueling swim; trying desperately to return them both to shore, not knowing if his friend may have already succumbed to the elements; praying he, himself wouldn't.

Patrick got within a few meters of the shore when another

rope was tossed to him. Barely having the strength, he held onto both ropes as he and Mike were pulled to safety. Patrick feverously got Mike loose from the ropes. He was still alive, gurgling, gasping for breath. Patrick rolled him over on his side and Mike ejected a gush of water and bile. After a few minutes, he was able to speak.

"I thought I was done for," he got out between coughs. "I thought I was alone and would bloody drown tied to that piece of ship," his voice raspy from the combination of bile and salt.

"You were never alone, Mike. I wasn't going to let you die tied to that thing. I tied you there, so I wouldn't lose you."

Both men were given warm blankets and helped to a wagon. The pungent odor of the wet oilcloth tarps which kept out the harsh rain and wind assaulted Patrick's nose. A large fire had been started with coal oil providing the welcomed heat and the firelight showing there were other survivors receiving care.

Someone handed Mike and Patrick cups of warm rum; only then did Patrick realize his hands were shaking.

Only twelve souls survived the night. Neither the ship's captain, any of the crew, nor Patrick's employer were among them. Fate had voided the dubious contract. Patrick was now on his own. No family, no money, and nowhere to turn in a strange, foreign land. The same fate that set him free would come with a cost. And fate always collected its debts.

William N. Gilmore

CHAPTER 4

Bill Warner was enjoying his new retirement. Now there was more time to spend with family, especially his grandson, and to do the things he put off for so long. After nearly thirty years on the Atlanta Police Department, he accumulated so many stories, he decided to try and write about some of them.

He had been lucky during his service; no critical injuries, no gunshot or knife wounds, and he was never put into a situation where he was forced to fire his weapon at any suspect.

Oh, there were plenty of fights while trying to make arrests and more than a couple of scrapes and bruises. He received his share of complaints about being too rough or making false arrests and even the bogus reports that he was on the take, but there was never anything sustained and there was a stack of commendations and awards to go along with top marks every year on his efficiency reports.

Now it was time to take a break. It surprised everyone when he announced his retirement, especially at such a young age. He was only fifty-three. He had been a main fixture in the detective squad for over twenty years and he was the guy to go to for the department's inside information. This was before any of those new-fangled computers the department bought. It sped up the work but made it much less personal. He could give you a suspect's name based just on the crime, the location, description, or weapon. He was a walking encyclopedia of the city's crime information. He was a resource which was going to be tough to lose and impossible to replace.

When Bill and his grandson left the coin store, he had a funny feeling. He paid attention to his feelings. It was one reason he made it to retirement.

"Gee, Grandpa Bill," Sam began with a sigh, "I sure would like to have a new bicycle," giving a slight down and sideways glance as his grandfather drove away from the store.

"I'm sure you would," Grandpa Bill said, "but I don't think you would have gotten the best of the deal. I think there's more to this coin than meets the eye."

"What do you mean, Grandpa?"

"He jumped his price up way too much from two hundred dollars to five hundred dollars in a hurry and saying things to try to get us to sell him the coin."

"You think it's worth more, Grandpa?"

"It's possible, but I think there's still more to it. Something's not right. It's time to do some detective work and find out what is really going on."

"Can I be a detective too?"

"Of course, you can. You are the lead detective. We wouldn't even have a case if you didn't find the coin."

"Oh, boy, can I—"

"No gun and no badge. We're doing this undercover. Tell no one, partner."

"Sure thing, partner," Sam said, with a huge grin.

William N. Gilmore

CHAPTER 5

Caution's tenth birthday party was an elaborate affair. Her father had hired a team to decorate the yard. Her mother made sure the finest baker in town made the biggest and prettiest cake of any birthday in memory.

The guest list included the families of high society, business, and finance. The only problem was Caution barely knew anyone on the list. She only recognized them from her school or her father's business dealings. There were a few older children she knew who accompanied their parents on rare occasions. To Caution, the party appeared to be more for her parents than for her. It was their idea. She didn't like being in a crowd of people. Especially, people she didn't have anything in common with.

She wished her Grandpa Patrick would come again soon. It seemed like such a long time since he made his last appearance. At times, she wondered if, as her mother suggested, her make-believe friends and playmates would one day leave and not return; that as she got older, she would not need them as much. She hoped her mother was wrong, at least for today. As she hid in her bedroom on her own birthday, she needed her grandpa more than ever.

*

Several months later, as Caution returned one day from school, her mother rushed her past the closed door of the study. Shouting and harsh words echoed from behind the closed door. This was not her father's voice; it was one she didn't recognize.

"Why is someone yelling at Daddy, Mother?" Caution asked, confusion ringing in her young voice.

"Oh, it's just a disagreement over some contracts," her mother lied. "They're not mad, they're just trying to get their point across. It's just business."

But Caution saw something in her mother's moistened eyes. Something she'd never seen before; fear.

A few days later, the family returned home from an early dinner engagement only to find that someone had forced their way into the home, ransacking it, primarily the study.

Police were called as a precaution to be sure no one was still on the premises. A patrol car arrived, emergency lights flashing in the night, giving a bluish hue to everything in sight. A second unit soon pulled into the driveway as back-up. The officers, having the owners remain at the front door, made a painstakingly, careful search to be sure there were no perpetrators remaining in the large house.

After making sure it was clear, the lead officer, following procedures, called for a crime scene investigation unit and a detective unit, although the husband seemed surprisingly hesitant to follow-up on the break-in.

Detective Vickie Winston arrived to conduct the investigation. The tall, shapely policewoman exhibited a confident look of professionalism with a get down to business attitude. Having been briefed by the uniformed officers, she directed the CSI team that just arrived to try to find fingerprints or any other physical evidence of the crime.

She met with the victims and after a quick tour of the house, she sat with the Murphy's to ask some of the routine questions related to the burglary.

"Have either of you noticed anything missing?" Detective Winston began, getting her notebook and pen ready. She was expecting a large list of items including cash, jewelry, and other valuables. She also expected the list to be padded as is often the case when there was going to be an insurance claim.

"Nothing's been taken that we can determine," Mr. Murphy stated, much to the detective's surprise. "We made a quick check of things after the officers made sure no one was still here."

"What time did you leave the house and what time did you return?" Winston continued.

"It was close to 6:00 p.m. when we left," Mrs. Murphy answered. "We got home about an hour ago; somewhere around 9 o'clock."

It was plain to Winston that whoever broke in had plenty

of time to get away with quite a bit if they had wished, but it was also obvious they seemed to be looking for something in particular.

"Do you have any idea who may have a reason to break in or what someone may have been after?"

"I imagine they were after something of value. Electronics, jewelry, something they could pawn or sell on the streets. Isn't that what they usually do?" Mr. Murphy asked, in a huff, getting a little perturbed at the questioning.

As the detective was talking with Mr. and Mrs. Murphy, Caution left her room and bounded down the stairs. Clutching one of her dolls, she sat with her parents.

"Hello, I'm Detective Winston," the pretty policewoman said, smiling and holding out her hand to Caution.

"Hello. I'm Caution Murphy," she said, taking the woman's hand.

"What an interesting name," Winston said, glancing over at the parents.

"It's something her grandmother always would say to her," her mother stated. "She was an exceedingly active baby, always kicking before she was even born and while I was on full bed rest. It seemed to calm her down, allowing me to relax and sleep. And the name stuck."

"Are you going to catch the people who robbed my house?" Caution asked.

"Well, I'm going to try to find out what happened," the detective said, taking another quick glance over at the parents. "Although, houses can't be robbed. It was what we call a burglary. That's when someone breaks into a house to steal something or to commit another crime. I'm sure it's a little scary to come home to something like this."

"Okay, Caution, let the detective do her job and then we'll clean up the mess," her father said, stealing another glance at the detective.

"But I'm not scared," Caution quickly exclaimed as she stood up. "I think it's exciting. Maybe one day I could be a detective too. Just like my Grandpa Patrick."

"Oh, so you have some law enforcement in the family?" the detective asked.

"Ah, no, not really," Mr. Murphy stumbled with the answer. Looking at his wife, he gave just a slight shake of his head. She furrowed her brow and shook her head as well. Mr. Murphy glanced over at his daughter who was playing with the doll's hair and said to the detective, "My great-grandfather, Patrick Murphy, was with the Pinkerton's at one time, but that's something we've never really discussed. Caution, how did you know about your great-great-grandpa being a detective?"

"Because he told me," she said innocently, straightening the doll's dress as she skipped out of the sitting room.

The long silence was broken as Detective Winston stood

and handed Mr. Murphy her business card. "Call me if you do find anything missing or have any questions. I'll see what our CSI team comes up with and have added patrols for the neighborhood start right away. I'll have a copy of the report for you by the end of the week."

"Thank you, Detective," the Murphy's said, in unison.

Winston went to check on the forensic team. Something was off. She could feel it. Usually, when victims were reluctant to be of much help it was because they were trying to hide some other illegal activity, protect someone, or distrusted the police. This didn't have that feel, but there was something.

The CSI team found no evidence of value, packed up their equipment, and left the scene. As Detective Winston left the house heading for her car, she looked back. From an upstairs window, she saw Caution smiling and waving at her. She waved back at the polite and strange little girl.

As she got to her car, she glanced back up and for an instant, she thought she saw the figure of a man standing behind Caution, a man who wasn't her father, but a long second look made her believe she was mistaken.

CHAPTER 6

Patrick, like many of the survivors, was taken in by one of the families of the village community for a few weeks until he was well enough to be on his own. He was lucky nothing was broken, and the many cuts and bruises healed quickly. When he was able, he helped with the chores, cutting firewood, feeding the animals, and hauling water to help repay the kindness shown to him. It was his way. It was his family's way.

While back in Ireland, when Patrick's parents became ill, he tried to care for them the best he could. The once prosperous business, another victim of the potato blight, was now almost in ruins. Patrick had worked himself to exhaustion trying to save both. He was unsuccessful.

His uncle, a farmer who lived many miles away with a small patch of land for growing barley and oats, took him in. Patrick was well taken care of, loved, educated, but he became restless. He didn't want to be a farmer or a weaver. He hoped for an adventure. He knew it was a gamble, but he left.

Now Patrick was on an adventure, maybe not the one he expected, nor the one he wanted, but the one he was handed.

One day while he was out chopping wood, a wagon rumbled up the dusty road and stopped at the house. There was a large trunk in the back. Patrick recognized it immediately.

Anything that could be identified was returned to the survivors or the families, if any, of the lost. The locked trunk was identified as his former employers by the monogram on its front. It had washed ashore about a week earlier.

The heavy wooden trunk was well made, sturdy and tight, with leather straps and ornate metal covering the corners. Surprisingly, there was minimal damage to it and he believed the saltwater had not gotten inside. Patrick was never allowed to see inside the trunk. The tailor was especially protective of his belongings, particularly his personal tools. Many of which were specially made. Now the tools and other contents belonged to Patrick.

Michael, from his gratitude or in some sense of loyalty for having saved his life, was at Patrick's side as often as he could be. He offered to help him with his chores every day after completing his own at the house where he was staying and if allowed, would have stayed with Patrick's foster family, but luckily for Patrick, there just wasn't room.

Michael happened to be there as the trunk was being delivered to Patrick. "That's a mighty fine-looking piece," Mike said, inspecting the case in the back of the wagon. "It looks heavy."

"It took two good sized men just to load it," the old wagon driver said, obvious he wouldn't be much help, even if he offered.

"Just where do you plan to store it?" Mike asked.

"For now, I think it will go in the barn until I figure what to do with it," Patrick stated. "You mind helping getting it in there?"

"Just step out of the way, so you don't get hurt," Michael said, brushing his arm out, scooting Patrick back a few steps. Michael grabbed the trunk, pulling it just over the edge of the back of the wagon. Grabbing one of the end straps, he pulled on the large trunk. Turning, bending over, and slightly bending his knees, he maneuvered his arm over his head and got the trunk onto his shoulders and back. "Well, are you going to just stand there gawking or are you going to show me where you want this monster?"

Patrick walked ahead of Mike to the barn, afraid he would hear the snap of either the strap or Mike's back. He directed Mike to the spot he wanted the trunk to sit and helped him with what he could to get the trunk down.

Mike stood upright and slowly bent backwards, a few bones giving a pop, and just as slowly straightened back up, shaking his arm out. "You might look to see if your hefty tailor didn't stuff himself into that trunk," Mike laughed.

Patrick had no desire at that time to open the trunk. It was a bitter-sweet moment. Knowing he was now free from a lifetime of servitude, he wondered what he was going to do with himself.

He knew all along he didn't want to follow his employer's trade as a tailor and thought he probably would sell the contents of the chest if they had any value but that would only last him so long.

Every day, Big Mike talked endlessly about the things he heard concerning California and all the gold and fertile land there. He loved to retell the stories he heard maybe third or fourth hand about gold nuggets as big as your fist which you could pluck out of shallow mountain streams.

Another was about a vein of gold in a mine which was as wide as a horse and ran halfway through the territory. His favorite though was one about a lush valley the Indians believed was sacred and was hidden until just as the sun was coming up in a certain place during a particular time of the year.

Just as the sun rose over the horizon, and if you were in the right spot, you would see it light the only passage to the valley for just a few seconds and shine on the protective mountain's walls of gold within. You would have to shade your eyes from the reflection of all the gold or go blind.

There were many such tales; mostly told by drunken old miners down on their own luck looking to get a drink from anyone who would listen. If the drinks continued to pour, the tales got bigger.

Some even possessed maps of Spanish treasure locations or lost mines they would reluctantly be willing to let go for a price. And there were those with visions of gold falling out of their over-stuffed saddle packs who were just gullible enough to believe them. Gold has a funny effect on people.

Michael didn't believe all of those wild treasure tales, but he believed enough of them to travel the nearly six-thousand miles from Ireland to California, and through all the hardships he endured so far, he was now finally in America, halfway there.

Although he lost all his belongings, including his savings in the shipwreck, he wasn't about to stop now, not this close, yet he felt a moral obligation to Patrick. Patrick saved his life after all and they were now best of friends. There was only one solution to this problem. "Take him to California with you," he said to himself and smiled, thinking maybe they could even be partners.

William N. Gilmore

CHAPTER 7

"What do we do first, Grandpa Bill?" Sam asked, ready to start his tenure as a young detective.

"I still have a few favors to cash in over at the police department. Tomorrow, let's go see if we can find out more about that Mr. Dearing at the coin store."

"He seemed nice, but you don't trust him, do you, Grandpa?"

"I'm just suspicious. It's years of having people tell me stories and trying to get away with things, and I don't think they are telling me all the truth."

"Like the time I told you I didn't know who broke the window in my bedroom. You knew I did it. It was an accident and I was scared, but you knew." Sam said, his head down.

"Yes, I knew. But you did the right thing and told the truth. Of course, which was later, and your mom punished you for not telling the truth right away."

"She would have punished me anyway."

"Maybe so, but she was more disappointed you lied. And *that* made it worse. A window can easily be replaced, but once a lie is told, it's hard to replace the broken trust."

*

Not long after the break-in at the house, Caution's father arrived home one weekend from a business trip with a surprise. He brought home a puppy. Well, it wasn't so much of a puppy anymore, but a young dog. He hoped it would grow to become Caution's close companion and protector. He wanted this dog to be young enough to be able to grow with Caution, but old enough to begin the duties of which he hoped would not be necessary; to protect Caution and be a deterrent for any other break-ins.

With the burglary at the house, knowing the police couldn't always be there to see to their safety and hiring private security while he was gone much of the time not a practical option, he wanted to know there was some dependable protection in the home. His wife wasn't real comfortable with firearms and with a young, curious child, he felt something else would be better for them.

He remembered the foreman of their country farm property telling him about his dog having puppies shortly after their last visit several months ago. All the puppies were given away except for two, leaving them to learn from their mother and some of the other dogs and trained to help look after the property and other animals.

Caution liked the dogs at the farm. They always came running up to her when she arrived. At one time, her father was reluctant to let her have a dog. He knew the care and responsibility might be too much for Caution, relying more on him and her mother to take care of it, as well as knowing how the dogs naturally preferred the open spaces of the farm. They weren't meant to be cooped up in a fancy house and restricted to an open, manicured backyard, but things change. Now, he felt she was ready, but more importantly, he was ready as well.

During the long drive home, he made the detour for the farm. He called his wife, telling her of his plans, but more to get permission than anything. She was quick to agree and believed it would be a wonderful idea, although her thoughts were more on how it might benefit Caution.

When her father arrived home with the dog, Caution was more than overwhelmed. The two took to each other immediately with the dog's tail wagging excitedly against Caution's legs as she circled around her. Caution's smile growing bigger every second as she petted and ran her hands through the dog's coat. The young dog, an obvious product of good breeding, appeared to sense the joy and seemed to be smiling as well.

"Oh, she's beautiful," Caution's mother beamed.

"Her name is Molly, but you can call her anything you want, sweetheart. She's yours now," her father said, standing next to his wife with his arm around her.

"That's a wonderful name." Caution declared. "No need to change it now. I'm sure she's used to it, aren't you Molly?"

The dog stopped, sat, and cocking her head with her ears

standing up, looking up at Caution as if to see what command she was about to give.

"Just like her mother, she's smart and quick to learn," Caution's father noted. "She'll need to get outside a lot. She's not the type of dog that will want to just sit in your lap or lay around. She'll need lots of exercise and attention and things to keep her busy. Do you think you can handle all of that?"

"She's not something to dress up or to toss aside when you're bored with her," her mother advised. "This is only a trial and if you aren't responsible enough, she goes back to the farm. Is that clear?"

"Yes, ma'am. May I take her outside, Father?"

"Of course, as a matter of fact, I think she may need to after the drive. Keep her on the leash though," he said, handing it over for her to attach to the collar, "until she gets used to the yard and the boundaries."

"And take a plastic bag to clean up," her mother added. "We don't want any accidents while we're walking in the yard."

"Oh, that's yucky," Caution said, making a sour face.

"Your dog, your mess," her father said, laughing.

After Caution went out to the backyard, her mother turned to her husband and asked, "Do you really think that dog will protect her? She's not very big and she's almost too cute."

"These dogs are fiercely loyal and incredibly protective. They're working dogs. They make sure the flock is where they are supposed to be and is out of danger. They'll even fight threatening wolves and coyotes. I didn't want to get a guard or attack type dog, one we would have to worry about hurting some innocent person or would be hard to handle. I think this is the best fit for all of us."

"Alright," his wife said with a half-smile. "I'm hoping this new responsibility will bring Caution out of her reclusiveness. It's time to put the dolls and imaginary friends away and get her out of her room."

William N. Gilmore

CHAPTER 8

"California?" Patrick repeated. "That's a long, bloody ways away. I hadn't planned on going to California."

"Well, what else are you going to be doing with yourself?" Big Mike asked. "Now that your poor, departed employer went and left you all alone with nothing but a bloody trunk full of needles and thread. You can sew yourself a mighty nice pouch, but you ain't even got a pretty rock to put in it. There's gold just waiting to be found and with the two of us together, we could have a fortune in no time. I even hear the Wee People are leaving their rainbows and headed to California to fill their pots."

"Now, I doubt that's for real," Patrick said, with a laugh. True enough, he didn't have any plans to go to California, but all the decisions for the near future were made for him by someone else. Now he needed to find a way to make it in America on his own, or maybe, not so alone after all.

"And just how are we supposed to make this long journey, on foot, horseback, or by ship, and with what money?"

"No damn ships," Big Mike said, with a cringe. "I don't ever want to be on the bloody water again."

Patrick laughed, nodding his head in agreement.

"There are wagons going all the time" Big Mike continued. "We can be there quick. Maybe in five and a half or six months. We can work our way there. Hire on as drivers, or cooks, or such. I even read there are women who need men to protect them and help with their teams."

"And what do you know about being a driver, much less cooking?" Patrick asked. "Both of us lost everything we came with except the clothing we had on and now, what we can borrow. We have no horses, supplies or even any guns to protect ourselves, much less women. They'd have to protect us. And you surely don't want to taste my cooking."

Big Mike lowered his head. He was heartbroken. His plans for a big future were smashed right along with the ship. Patrick could see he wasn't helping by being overly honest as the big guy's shoulders drooped from near total defeat and his eyes got that empty, hollow look. This was a man about to find out his lifelong dreams were now worthless fantasies.

"But then again," Patrick said as he shook his head. "What the bloody hell am I going to do with myself anyway? Count me in."

Big Mike looked up. His eyes widened as a big smile came over his youthful face. He reached out and grabbed Patrick who was also smiling, lifting him up into a near crushing bear hug. Now, they were partners.

CHAPTER 9

Before there was even a knock at the front door, Molly ran downstairs. Caution was not far behind. Molly took a frozen stance, staring at the door as if it were a living thing, ready to pounce on it or whatever came through it which posed any danger. A soft growl grew in the dog's throat as Caution caught up with her.

"It's okay, Molly," Caution said, looking through the pulled back curtains of a nearby window. The automatic outside lights just came on in the early twilight. "It's just that nice policewoman." Molly, sensing Caution's ease, ceased her growl and sat, but didn't take her eyes off the door.

With barely any time for the detective to knock, Caution opened the door and with a big smile, greeted the woman.

"Hi, Detective Winston. Did you catch the robber—oops, I mean the burglar who broke into my house?"

"No, I'm sorry, not yet."

Caution's mother came to the front foyer from the kitchen. "I'm sorry, Detective, I didn't hear you at the door."

"Caution was quick on the draw and opened it before you could say 'lickity split'. I barely made contact with the door."

"Molly knew she was here before I did," Caution said,

showing pride in her.

"Oh, I didn't know you owned a dog," the detective stated.

"She's a new addition to the family because of the other night. New here, anyway. She was born at our property in the country. We thought she would be a good distraction for Caution and she is extremely keen and obviously very protective." Molly was now standing in front of Caution, between her and the detective with her ears straight up and her bright eyes fixed on the woman.

"That's really good. I hope I wasn't catching you at a bad time, but I was just on my way home after getting off and wanted to stop by. Ah, could I have a moment to talk to you and your husband about your case? In private if you don't mind."

"Sure, but Mr. Murphy hasn't gotten home yet if that's alright." Mrs. Murphy said, eyeing the detective for just a second before turning to Caution. "Take Molly out to the backyard, dear. And don't forget to clean up after her," she added.

"I won't, Mother," Caution said, with a sigh. "Come on girl, let's go play in the back." Caution began to run off towards the rear of the house and Molly, giving the detective a second look, ran to catch up with her young owner.

"Come into the kitchen," Mrs. Murphy said. "Would you like some coffee or something else to drink?"

"Coffee would be fine, thank you," said Detective

Winston. "I hadn't heard from you and just wanted to check to see if there was anything else you wanted to add to the report before I turned it in."

Mrs. Murphy pulled down a mug from a cupboard, "Cream? Sugar?"

"No, black is just fine."

"I'm sorry I don't have any doughnuts or anything much right now. I haven't done the shopping yet."

The detective gave a little laugh. "Yes, it's true. We cop's do love our doughnuts and our coffee," she said, as she received the mug of coffee from Mrs. Murphy. "Thank you."

"So, are there any ideas about who might have broken into our house?" Mrs. Murphy asked.

"Oh, your house? Caution indicated it was her house."

They both gave a little chuckle. The detective was trying to get Caution's mother to feel at ease and keep the conversation light for a bit. It was one of her usual tactics when speaking with victims and suspects. It might get them to talk a little easier and maybe say something that otherwise might not come out.

"Mmm. This is really good coffee," the detective said. "Did you grind it yourself or do you have a special blend?"

Mrs. Murphy, from years in big business and dealing with corporate people, knew exactly what the detective was doing. But that was fine with her.

"It's Costa Rican. So, when you were here last, you said

you would check again with your forensic team to see if they found anything. Did they?"

"Unfortunately, not. But that only tells me whoever broke in knew what they were doing. Possibly a professional making it look like a typical break-in. There were no fingerprints; no footprints, nothing left behind, all of which is unusually rare. However, nothing was taken, which is also not typical. Or, reported to have been taken," she added for effect and to see if there was any reaction from Mrs. Murphy. "There haven't been any other burglaries in this neighborhood for years. So, what do you think someone would be after?" she asked, as she took a long sip of the coffee, staring over the rim of the mug at Mrs. Murphy.

"I have no idea," Mrs. Murphy said, stone-faced. "We don't keep any large amounts of cash lying around and I have only a few pieces of jewelry here which might be considered valuable. The valuable items are in a safety deposit box at the bank. I'm just not into that kind of stuff. No furs or fine art. There aren't any real collections in the house other than my husband's historical documents he collects. It's a hobby of his. Things from around the mid-1800's, early settlers, and the Civil War mostly. He's thinking about writing a book on the era when he retires."

"Would that have anything to do with his grandfather? The one who was with the Pinkerton's?" Detective Winston inquired.

"Oh, I'm sure there will be a good bit about him." Mrs. Murphy added.

"Correct me if I'm wrong, but Caution is only what, nine or ten years old?"

"She's ten now."

"There's little chance her great-great-grandfather was still alive when she was born, is there?"

"No. He had been gone for many years by then. Even before I was born. I think I understand why you are asking. Caution has an extremely vivid imagination and loves to make up stories. I think it's because she has no real friends or playmates around. Like many children around her age, she also makes up invisible friends. So, the other day when she said her Grandpa Patrick told her he was a detective, I think it was just a coincidence. The fact that you were here as a detective, she somehow correctly said her Grandpa Patrick was also a detective. She might even have overheard her father and I talk about it at one time or her father forgot he may have said anything. A lot of his notes are about his grandfather and there are even some old pictures, letters, and a journal he kept."

"When I was leaving the other day," The detective added, "Caution was waving to me from an upstairs window. I could have sworn I saw a man standing behind her at one point."

"I'm sure you were mistaken," Mrs. Murphy concluded.

"There's just the three of us, oops, four of us in the house now that Molly has joined us. Both my husband and I were downstairs after you left. Maybe it was a shadow or the light playing tricks on you."

"Possibly. This is a large house and yard and you said there were no housekeepers, maids, gardeners, or any other help. Forgive me for asking, but why not? It appears you are financially well off and can afford it?"

"We used to have a small staff before Caution was born and shortly thereafter, but good help was hard to keep. Since my husband is so successful, and it takes him away much of the time, I decided I wanted to be here for my daughter. So, I quit the corporate world and now, I take care of her and the house. I enjoy it."

Detective Winston got back to the point of her visit. "You never did say if there was anything you wanted to add to the report. Did you find anything missing?"

"No. There's nothing to add."

"Is there anything you might want to change?"

"What are you getting at, detective?" Mrs. Murphy asked. "We told you just the way things happened."

"Sometimes," Detective Winston explained, "after a couple days, you remember things a little differently, or you see things a little clearer. I don't mean to insinuate anything. I just want everything to be right before I turn in the official report."

"Well, Detective, I'm sure you've written a glowing report. It seems the only thing to do now is to find out who broke into our house," Mrs. Murphy said. "Or would that be too much of a bother?"

Detective Winston kept her cool. She was a professional and benefited from years of experience in interviews and interrogations. "Oh, it's no bother; in fact, it's my job to cover all the angles and to investigate the crime fully, no matter where it leads."

This time, it was Mrs. Murphy who played it cool. "Good. Just as long as we know where we both stand. More coffee?" she asked, with a smile.

William N. Gilmore

CHAPTER 10

The next day, Grandpa Bill picked up Sam at his house and after a nice breakfast at their favorite pancake shop, they headed for downtown Atlanta.

"Detective Warner, it's good to see you. How's retirement treating you?" the tech at the police department's identification section asked.

"It's going well, Carrie. Much less stress," Bill returned.

"And who is this handsome young man?"

"This is my grandson, Sam."

"Grandpa!" Sam exclaimed, glancing up with a hurt look.

"Oh, I'm sorry," Bill began again after a wink at Carrie, "this is my partner, Detective Sam."

"Well, then you must be the youngest detective on the force. I'm ID Tech Flowers, but you may call me Carrie," she said as she offered her hand over the counter. Sam, just barely tall enough to see over the counter, took her hand and smiled.

"You must be on a very important case," she said with a serious look at Sam. "What can I do for you, Detectives?" Carrie said, giving a wink back at Bill.

Bill pulled out his handkerchief and reached into his shirt pocket. He pulled out a small plastic case that he held by the edges and placed it on the counter. "We need to get a fingerprint from this case and run it for identification."

The ID Tech looked at Bill and smiled as she shook her head. "I wish I could Bill, but you're no longer active duty."

"Technically, I'm in the reserves, I still have a badge," Bill said.

"But it could still get me in hot water with the brass if they knew."

"Well then, we just won't tell them. Just like the time we didn't tell them about you showing up to work on a crime scene after an extended night out; just a little unsteady and throwing up on some evidence as I recall," he said smiling.

She looked down at Sam, red-faced and giving a forced smile. "I'll be right back with my fingerprint kit."

Carrie returning after a few moments wearing some latex gloves and wielding a much-used brush. She opened a jar containing some fine, black powder and dipped the brush into it and tapped it against the side. She lightly twirled the brush over the plastic case and then flipped it over and did the same to the other side. "That's a beautiful coin," she said.

"I found it," Sam said, standing on his tip toes to see the process.

"Oh, so this is a lost and found case. Now I see," she said, continuing her work.

"I found it—" Sam started.

"That's right, Sam," his grandpa jumped in before he got any further. "You found it," he said as he patted the boy on the head and letting his open hand slide down to cover the boy's mouth. Sam looked up and Grandpa Bill was shaking his head.

"There's a really good thumbprint on the case," Carrie said. "Should be quick and easy to find who you are looking for now with these newer computers. I'm sure they will be happy to get the coin back." Looking at Sam, she continued. "Good thing we had a good and honest detective like Sam to find it." The tech then took some wide fingerprint tape and placed it over the print on the case, pressing down and all around to make sure the powder adhered to the tape, she lifted the print and placed it on a fingerprint card. She handed the case back to Bill who wiped the residual powder off and put it back into his shirt pocket. "I'll classify this," she said smiling, "and see if I can find a match. Shouldn't be too long."

Bill and Sam went into the sitting area where there were a number of customers waiting to get fingerprinted for various reasons; a bartending permit, a stripper for a dance permit, a taxi driver, and a young, big, burly guy getting a permit to be a tow truck driver.

As they sat down, the big guy said, "You got to get a number," pointing over to a ticket dispenser.

"Thanks, but we've already been waited on," Bill said. "How'd you do that? I've been here almost an hour and they still haven't called my number. What number did you have?"

"We didn't need a number. This is special business," Bill said, quietly.

"We're detectives," Sam said, not so quietly.

Bill looked around and saw several smiles and more than a few quizzical expressions on the faces of some of the customers. He smiled back and just shook his head.

"I'm Bubba, Bubba Thompson," the big guy said to Sam. "I'm going to be a tow truck driver."

"I'm Sam. Detective Sam."

"Excuse us just a minute," Bill said. "Sam, let's go get some water over at the fountain in the hallway."

Sam followed Grandpa Bill into the hallway where his grandpa stopped before getting to the water fountain. Turning to the young boy he said, "Sam, you can't keep telling people you are a detective. Remember what I said? We're undercover. We can't keep blowing our cover. If you happen to tell the wrong person, it could stop us from investigating this case, or at least, I would have to do it without you, and I don't want to do that. I need you. You're my partner and partners have each other's backs."

"I'm sorry, Grandpa. I'm just so proud to be a detective and to be your partner. I'll do better."

"I know you will. I'm proud to have you as my partner. I'm not mad or anything, but let's just try really hard to say as little as possible to anyone else about what we are doing. Okay?"

ID Tech Flowers came into the hallway. "Bill, may I speak with you a moment, please? Alone."

William N. Gilmore

CHAPTER 11

Big Mike walked around all day with as big a grin as could fit his face. Patrick, on the other hand, expressed a bit of a worried look. He still didn't know how they were going to be able to get all the way to the other side of this vast country.

They had no money to speak of and there just weren't any real prospects to make any. It would take a lot just to get to California and then once there, Big Mike's grandiose plan was to become prospectors. As with almost any fortune-hunting adventure, you had to have money to make money. Or, as it was in most cases, you had to have money to kiss it goodbye.

Patrick finished his chores for the day and went into the barn where the big wooden trunk, once the property of the lonely tailor, sat. It now belonged to Patrick. He went over to it and looked at the sturdy integrated lock. There were not any keys among the recovered belongings of the tailor.

Patrick almost hated having to break the lock, but there might be some things inside he could sell; some cloth, sewing needles, scissors, maybe even a few silver thimbles like the one he first found on the tailor's floor way back in his home country.

Patrick got a hammer and chisel and placed the chisel along the top of the mechanism of the lock where it was flush with the chest and raised the hammer.

"Whoa! What do you think you're doing there, lad?" Big Mike said as he walked into the barn.

"I'm going to open the chest and see if there is anything we can sell. We're going to need money, you know," Patrick returned, starting to raise the hammer again.

"So, you're going to destroy the one thing that you know you have just to see if there is something inside that you don't.?"

"What?" Patrick slowly lowered the hammer. "Just what the bloody hell are you trying to say?"

"This chest might be just as valuable or more so as anything inside. Look at how she's made, how she survived the journey, the sea. She has a life of her own. She has a destiny." Sometimes, and they were rare, Big Mike exhibited moments of sheer brilliance. "Let me have a go at that lock before you ruin the whole bloody thing. I didn't want to say at our first meeting," he said, giving a sheepish grin, "but I seem to have a way with things that are locked."

"You have a way with locked things, you say? And just how did you come to have this—gift?" Patrick inquired, his head cocked to one side and now his hands on his hips. "Did you happen to catch one of the Wee People and he gave you some special lessons or provide you with a pinch of magic dust in exchange for his release? Or, most likely the answer is you just somehow found yourself in need and were forced to learn on your own to survive."

"We all have to do the things we do to survive," Big Mike said, losing the grin. "Some things come naturally, others are easy to learn, some hard, most come out of necessity, and still there are the others that are unspeakable."

"You're talking about the gangs, aren't you?" Patrick asked, but not waiting for an answer. "I've heard about what some gangs do. They teach you to steal and fight. How to do it without getting caught. How cruel some of the leaders are and what they do if you don't steal enough or try to run away. And what they do to you if you do get caught and squeal."

"It kept me alive for a number of years." Big Mike said, remembering. "I was taught by one of the best at picking locks and getting into safes. I was good. But that was a past life. And now I am going to get your permission to pick the lock on your trunk. That will be a first for me. It's been a while, but I think I can still impress you. And then I'll be able to fashion you a key, so you can still lock it and unlock it when you wish.

"What would be the point with you around?" Patrick laughed.

"I'll be right back, I have to get a few things before I get started," he said, the grin having returned.

Patrick sat on a pile of hay to await Big Mike. He remembered about the gangs. His big brother, Aaron, had been part of one, the Liberty Boys. When Patrick was growing up, he asked about them, thinking it would be great to be part of something along with his brother. Aaron knocked him down, telling him to stick to his learning and his books and to forget the gangs, never to ask about them again. He told Patrick they were mean and cruel and if anyone ever tried to get him interested in one of the gangs, to tell him and he would deal with it.

The exciting thoughts of the gangs kept with young Patrick until the day Aaron was stabbed during a fight with a rival gang member. He lingered for days in pain, barely conscious, moaning. The infection from the dirty, and possibly intentionally infected blade, took over his body with great speed. Arron died a week later. The fight was started over nothing more than a rival gang member walking through an area claimed by the other gang.

During one of Aaron's few lucid moments, he blamed himself for getting stabbed. He had been surprised and noticed too late that the other guy was left handed. He got Patrick to promise he would never join a gang and would not seek revenge against the Ormond Boys or the guy with the big knife for his stabbing him. Since that time, Patrick no longer looked at the gangs as anything but a pox on the world.

Big Mike returned with several instruments. A couple were ground and remodeled horseshoes that appeared to have been made into picks. He also possessed a few small wires and pieces of metal in strange shapes. The tools of the trade.

He went over to the trunk, pulled it into some light and choosing one of the tools, began to work on the lock. Just as he began his work, Patrick came and stood over him. Big Mike stopped, slowly turning his head.

"If the sun could shine through you, I might be able to see what I'm bloody well doing, but if you are going to stand right there, I'm going to have to wait until tomorrow to get the right light again."

"I'm sorry, I'll move," he said as he went over to Big Mike's other side. "Do you know how long it might take?"

Mike turned completely around this time, looking Patrick right in the eyes.

"Well now, it looks like it just might take a long bloody while with all the interruptions. Why don't you tell me when you want me to do this?"

"Okay. I'm sorry," Patrick said, throwing up his hands and backing off. "I'll come back later to see if you have any luck."

"Don't go far, and lucks got nothing to do with it," Mike said, turning back to his work.

Patrick walked out of the barn, tilted his head, holding his face up to the warm sun. After just a short while, he lowered his head, rubbed his eyes and began to walk over to the well. He had just pumped the handle a few times to get the water flowing when Big Mike joined him.

"Taking a break so soon?" Patrick asked. "Or are you giving up already?" he continued as Mike cupped his hands for the cool water flowing out of the pump.

"It's done," Big Mike said.

Patrick stopped pumping. "What do you mean, it's done?"

"Done. Open. Unlocked. Done," Big Mike said.

"Did you break it open?" Patrick cringed, his eyes widening.

"Of course not," Big Mike huffed. "You do know what 'unlocked' means?"

"Did you see what's in it?" Patrick asked.

"No. That's not up to me. It be your chest. You have the honor," Mike said, bowing with a wave of his arm towards the barn.

"Well, let's go see what treasure awaits," Patrick said, cupping a handful of water from the pump and dowsing his face. He wiped his hands on his pants and headed back to the barn. Mike was right behind him.

CHAPTER 12

Mrs. Murphy and Detective Winston were just finishing their coffee when the phone rang. As Mrs. Murphy answered it, Caution and Molly came back into the kitchen.

"You and Mom are friends now," Caution said to the detective, smiling, seeing the coffee cups. "That's great. I hope you come by a lot. I want to hear about being a policeman, oops, I mean a policewoman."

"Well, I just came for an official visit. We're not really friends. It's that–"

"Who? Ah, yes, that's me." There was a slight pause. "Oh, no!" Mrs. Murphy cried, nearly dropping the phone.

Detective Winston, Caution, and even Molly turned to see what the exclamation was about.

"How badly is he hurt? What hospital? Okay, I'm on my way." Mrs. Murphy hung the phone up and turned, her face was flushed.

"Is everything okay?" Detective Winston asked, knowing the answer already.

"Mom?" Caution questioned. Even Molly, feeling the worry and concern, gave a soft whine.

"It's my husband. He was assaulted leaving the office.

Mugged. He may have a concussion and is being treated at Grady Hospital. I need to go."

"Would you like me to take you?" Detective Winston offered.

"Thank you, but they said I might be able to bring him home. I hate to ask something else of you though."

"Whatever I can do to help," the detective said.

"Would you mind staying with Caution right now? I don't think I can get anyone else here quickly and I have to leave right now."

The detective was caught off guard. "Well, she could go with you, couldn't she?"

Mrs. Murphy looked at Caution, hoping she would understand as well. "I don't think that would be a good idea. They don't like children in certain areas this late and I can't leave her alone in the waiting area. Please, I need to go now though."

"Yeah. Okay, sure." The detective gave-in in the face of the untimely emergency. "Just call me and let me know as soon as you find out something."

"Mom, is Daddy going to be alright?"

"Yes dear, I'm sure of it. They're taking good care of him. I just need to go and be with him and bring him home when he's ready. I'll call and tell you what's happening when I can. Don't worry, everything's going to be fine. You do what

Detective Winston says and get ready for bed."

"But I won't be able to sleep."

"Well, okay, but no television," she said, bending down giving her daughter a hug and a kiss before leaving.

Mrs. Murphy grabbed her car keys off a hook and started out the door, stopped and looked back. "Thank you, Detective. Looks like we owe you again. We'll talk more when this is over."

"No problem. I just hope everything's okay. Don't hurry on my account. We'll get along just fine."

Mrs. Murphy smiled and nodded as she headed out the door. Caution rushed to the window to watch her mother drive off. As the taillights went out of sight, her eyes filled with tears.

"I'm sure he's going to be alright," Detective Winston said, trying to sound convincing and reassuring at the same time, although not knowing even as much as Mrs. Murphy did from the short phone call.

"Yes. I hope so," Caution said, her voice cracking just a bit. She turned, and a few tears were running down her cheek. She ran and grabbed the detective as hard as she could, burying her face into the woman's body and began sobbing. Molly, sensing the emotionally troubled pair, whined and went and stood next to both Caution and the detective.

*

Bill left Sam in the waiting area and went to the counter.

"What's up, Carrie? Did you find something?"

ID Tech Flowers placed a thick folder on the counter in front of Bill. "This isn't a lost and found case after all, is it?"

"I never said it was. Sam did find the coin though, during our vacation."

"How did this guy get his prints on it?" She asked. "He's bad news."

Bill gave Carrie some of the information as he opened the file. There was a picture of the coin dealer staring back at him in a mug-shot photo. Tom Dearing was just one of the many names he used. His criminal history report was extensive and included charges and convictions on counterfeiting, theft, fraud, extortion, and assault, just to name a few. He served several stints in prisons out west and was currently out on parole. Receiving permission from the parole board, he moved to the Atlanta area. New state, new town, same old habits.

"So, what are you going to do now, Bill?" Carrie asked.

"I'm not sure. He hasn't broken any laws I know of and he appears to be running a legit shop, but then again, it's hard for a leopard to change its spots. I have some more research to do on this coin. I'm going to take it to another dealer. One I'll check out before I go."

"Good idea," Carrie agreed, "but what about your grandson? Please tell me you're not going to put him in any danger."

"Of course not. I'm just letting him have some fun and we're able to spend time together. It's been a while since we shared some good quality time, just him and me. I think it's good for both of us and it gives his mom a break."

"Then I think you did the right thing, retiring," Carrie said, nodding her head. "Nothing's more important than family."

William N. Gilmore

CHAPTER 13

Patrick entered the barn and went over to the chest. He looked at the lock and it was not damaged. The leather straps were unfastened, and he checked the heavy curved top and sure enough, it lifted, although with some effort, but it was not locked.

The top opened to a point where inside straps on both sides kept it from falling all the way back. There did not appear to be any water or even any moisture on the inside at all. The seal had been that good even after the rough ride it got in the sea and in its beaching. The trunk was obviously custom made for the tailor and it most certainly was not cheap, either.

The inside of the trunk was lined with a fine, light print material covering a sturdy metal frame. The top itself contained a special section to hold things. There was a top cloth cover Patrick pulled back and found there were sections to the trunk and several pullouts.

The top shelf of the trunk held a number of materials and cloths as he expected to find. One of the smaller pullouts held a large variety of needles. Another possessed scissors and small knives. There was an additional section just for threads. There was even a small section containing several of the small silver thimbles.

"Do you think we could get much for those?" Big Mike asked, standing over Patrick.

Patrick slowly turned his head towards Big Mike. "I don't think the bloody sun can shine through you either. Give me a chance to see what's here."

Big Mike backed off, but not too far. His curiosity peaked, and he wanted to see just what the trunk held as well.

Patrick continued to slowly go through the contents. The top inside shelf had handles on each side and it lifted straight up to reveal other sections with more rolls of cloth and apparently pre-made linings for vests and jackets.

Lying on top was a leather-bound book, held closed by several small straps. Patrick untied the straps and upon opening the book, found it was in-fact a journal with blank pages, ready for someone to give an account of their adventures.

Under that was a long, white belt, too short to be an apron. It was divided into sections with pockets covered by flaps. The sections bulged out a bit. It might be holding more needles and threads, Patrick surmised.

Patrick lifted it up and was surprised by its weight. It was unusually heavy. Then it hit him what kind of belt it was. He sat right down with the belt in his lap. Almost too scared to open one of the flaps.

"What ya got there, laddie, some more bloody sewing

needles?" Mike inquired.

It took Patrick a few seconds to answer. "I—I don't think so, Mike. I may have just found our way to California," he said, a little shaky, feeling the belt.

"You found a map, now did you?" Big Mike guessed badly.

"No, not a map. Something just a little better," Patrick said, as he turned, holding out his hand with a pile of gold British sovereign coins in it.

Big Mike's eyes widened as big as horseshoes and stared at the golden hoard. "Janey Mack! You found the end of the bloody rainbow," Big Mike barely got out, before dropping to his knees.

William N. Gilmore

CHAPTER 14

Caution stopped crying and was calming down some, however, she was still worried about her father and it took a long time for her to let go of Detective Winston.

"Are you hungry, dear?" the detective asked.

"No. Well, yes and no. My tummy feels funny and I'm afraid if I eat something, it might come back up."

"Okay then," the detective said, not wanting to push the issue, "why don't we just wait a bit and I'll see what there is to fix."

"Do you think it will be very long?"

"Whenever you're ready, sweetie."

"No, I mean for my mom to call. To say they're on the way home." It looked like Caution might start to cry again.

Detective Winston smiled and began with a calm, understanding tone. "The doctors are going to make sure your father is well enough to come home and then they have to do some paperwork, so sometimes it takes a little while before they can leave. They may even be here before you go to bed."

"May I go upstairs for a bit? "Caution asked, "I need to do something."

"Okay, but don't be too long. I'll get lonely down here,"

Detective Winston said, trying to lighten the conversation.

"Molly will stay with you, won't you girl?" Molly just cocked her head and stared at Caution. "I'll be right back. Stay girl." Caution took off upstairs.

Detective Winston poured herself another cup of coffee as she looked at the dog. Molly just sat where she was. After a short while, she said to the dog, "Okay Molly, go play." She made a motion with her hand as for the dog to go, but Molly continued to sit there looking at the detective. "Where's your toy, girl? Do you have a toy?" Detective Winston tried, but again, the dog just sat there. "Where's Caution? Go find Caution." Molly turned her head and looked up, but otherwise, didn't move. "I give up," she said, and headed for the living room.

Detective Winston had gone through the house once before, on the night of the burglary, and found it very lovely. She wandered around again, taking in the decor more this time than when she was doing the initial investigation. She was impressed with how well the house was decorated and maintained. There was no dust or clutter anywhere although every room felt more lived in than just a showplace.

When she came to the study, which was really more of a large office, she stopped at the doorway and took an extended time looking in, trying to imagine if there was something of interest to more than just an ordinary burglar. She went in and turned on the light.

At the desk were possibly important papers, business or personal finance records that could lead to identity fraud, something that was just beginning to make a mark on society; corporate secrets or plans someone could use for insider trading or even blackmail.

There was a trunk sitting on one side of the room. It was a big, beautiful, old thing. Obviously well made; sturdy looking and most likely, highly expensive, even in its day. She bet if it could talk it could tell some stories.

She wondered over to it, running her hands over the weathered wood and leather. She tested the lid and found it not locked. The heavy lid made her use two hands and took some effort to open, but she got it up. The inside of the trunk was just as beautiful as the outside, but it appeared to be empty. She began to lower the lid and the weight got the best of her. Letting it drop the last few inches before it caught her fingers, it slammed shut with a bang.

"Maybe somewhere in the room was a hidden safe even the police weren't told about. Could there be a secret panel? Okay, Winston, you're doing it again," she said to herself, shaking her head. *"You're over the top once more. Winston to Earth, beam me home, I've drifted too far out into space again."*

She started to turn to leave and as she did, she spotted something near the far corner of the room she hadn't noticed before. There were some pictures and documents in frames that appeared really old. Tintypes she believed the pictures were called. At least a hundred years of age and possibly much more. Some of the accompanying framed documents were slightly torn or faded but were still legible. The name on some of those documents was Patrick Murphy. That was Mr. Murphy's great-grandfather as she recalled.

She took a closer and longer look at one of the antique black and white photographs. It was a man in a uniform; military or police, she didn't know, but the face, something about the face. Then it hit her, and she quickly stepped back. It was the face of the man she saw standing behind Caution as she waved from the window!

CHAPTER 15

There were three of the money belts in the chest, each containing over fifty of the small, beautiful gold coins with the likeness of a young Queen Victoria. Under the belts were a number of tied draw-bags containing coins. Patrick counted out all the coins and stacked them on a board.

Big Mike kept going to the entrance of the barn to make sure no one came upon them and discovered the secret. He never stayed at the entrance long though, he would go back and look at the coins over and over again, watching as more stacks were added, hoping each time they would still be there and that this was real.

"I was wrong," admitted Big Mike, looking over his shoulder from the barn door. "The tailor left you a lot more than just needles and threads."

"Very true," Patrick was quick to agree. "But you know what else, Mike?"

"Did you find something more?" Mike's eyes got bigger, looking at the chest.

"Not so far," Patrick said. "But I was thinking, and I don't know why I didn't think of it before. The tailor was a fairly wealthy man. I can't imagine he left much of anything behind in

Ireland."

"Maybe he was wearing a belt or two himself when the ship went down," Big Mike suggested. "Could be why he hasn't been found. The weight kept him under."

"That's very possible," Patrick agreed. "But also, as I recall, this wasn't the only baggage he brought with him."

"You mean there could be more?" Mike exclaimed.

"Lots more," Patrick stated. "There were several trunks he brought on with him. Not as nice nor as big as this one. But they were all heavy and he kept them locked and close by."

"Do you think they survived the shipwreck?" Mike asked.

"It's doubtful. They may have sunk to the bottom or more likely, got smashed open and everything is spread along the ocean floor. Too deep to recover."

"That's a bloody shame now, isn't it?" Mike said. "But we should be grateful for what we have. I mean—for what we, ah—what I'm trying to say is—for what you have received."

Patrick laughed. "I know what you meant. We're in this together."

CHAPTER 16

A little shaken, Detective Winston wasn't really sure about what she thought she saw. Usually very confident and as a trained observer with years of experience, she rarely doubted herself. But this was just too weird.

She turned off the light as she left the study making her way back to the kitchen. Molly was curled up in the same spot she left her, but the dog sat up, watching her as she came into the room. Caution was not there and apparently was still up in her room. The detective went over to the refrigerator, opening the door to see what she might fix Caution to eat. As she scanned the fridge, and with the experience of a few minutes ago still burning on her brain, she jumped as her phone rang.

Fumbling to get her phone out, the detective laughed at herself before gaining control of it and answering, "Winston here."

"Detective, this is Mrs. Murphy."

"Yes, Mrs. Murphy. How is your husband?"

"He's going to be alright. No concussion, thank goodness, but a few stitches and a bit of a headache. They are going to discharge him soon, but it may still take an hour or so. I hope you don't mind. Is Caution behaving?"

"Oh, yes. She was a little worried earlier, but I think we got through that. She's up in her room right now. I'll tell her in a minute that you both will be back a little later. That should perk her up a bit."

"Thank you so much for doing this. You've gone way beyond the call of duty. We won't forget it."

"Don't mention it," Winston stated. "Just chalk it up as another public service of your police department. Just don't tell them about it."

"But you're off duty and it was kind of thrown in your face. Do you have a family, detective?"

She hesitated just a bit. "I'm on my own now. I devote most of my time to my job," Winston explained.

"Here comes the nurse with some more paperwork," Mrs. Murphy stated. "We should be home before it gets too late. Thanks again."

"You're welcome, Mrs. Murphy," Detective Winston said, adding, "Drive carefully", before disconnecting.

Winston thought she would let Caution know her dad was alright, and he and her mom would soon be on their way home. She went up the stairs and as she got to Caution's closed bedroom door, she thought she heard Caution talking. She believed Caution might have been on her own phone or even talking to one of her dolls. She knocked on the door and called out the child's name.

"Caution, I just spoke to your mom. I have some good news for you."

Caution opened the bedroom door, a big smile on her face. "My father isn't hurt too bad. He and Mom will be on the way home soon."

"That's right," Detective Winston confirmed. "Did she call you too?"

"No," Caution said, shaking her head. "I don't have a phone in my room."

"Oh, then you overheard me talking with her?"

"No. I just—know."

"Yes," Winston said, thinking she understood now. "It's good to have faith things will turn out for the best. Never lose hope."

"I prayed for Father earlier," Caution admitted, "but then I found out he was alright and coming home."

"How did you find that out?" Winston asked, her eyebrows furrowed, and wrinkles appeared on her forehead. She gazed around the child's room, not seeing evidence of anyone else.

"I'm not supposed to tell," Caution whispered.

William N. Gilmore

CHAPTER 17

"Five hundred and fourteen," Patrick said, placing the last coin on top of a stack.

"How much is that in American money?" asked Big Mike. "Is that enough to get to California?"

"I'm not sure," Patrick said, shrugging his shoulders. "I guess the best thing to do is to go into town and find a store or a bank to find out. But before we do, I want you to promise you won't say anything to anyone about this."

"Well," Mike started, "there is this pretty bird that I—"

"Mike!"

"I'm just kidding with you," Mike snickered. "Who am I going to bloody tell?" he said, throwing up his hands.

"That's just it," Patrick said. "You'll talk to anyone who will give you half an ear. This stays between us, or the deal is off and you're on your own. Understand?"

"I promise," Mike said, crossing his heart. "It doesn't leave this cake-hole."

"I've got to hide this somewhere," Patrick said, looking around the barn.

"Why not just put it back in the trunk and lock it?" asked Mike.

"That's just it. It's too obvious. That would be the first place anyone looking for anything I might have would look. Grab that spade over there and dig a hole in the far corner," he told Mike, pointing. "Dig it deep."

Patrick placed the coins that would fit, back into the bags and for those that wouldn't, he pulled one of the pieces of cloth out of the trunk, spread it out and placed the coins into it, tying the four corners together.

"Is this deep enough?" asked Big Mike.

"Would you want your future relying on that little divot?" Patrick asked, "because it just might, and then where would you be?"

Big Mike continued until there was a hole almost a foot deep. He looked up with a smile. "That should keep them safe."

Patrick put the bags and the tied cloth full of coins in the hole and Mike covered them up, spreading the remaining dirt around and for good measure, put some loose hay over the now invisible dig site.

"We'll go to town in a couple days and take just a few coins with us to see what we can get," Patrick suggested. "I don't want to let the word get out we have these. We could get robbed or even worse."

"That's smart," Mike agreed. He couldn't stop the grin that was coming. "How soon do you think we can start for California?"

"While we're in town," Patrick said, his own smile showing through, "we'll make some inquiries. See just what it takes to get there." He saw the look in Big Mike's eyes and backed up. He didn't want to get swallowed up in another bear hug.

CHAPTER 18

Winston was in the sitting room looking at a magazine when Caution came back downstairs a short time later. She decided not to press the young girl about what she meant earlier, not really knowing her and feeling she might still be upset with what happened to her father.

"How about I make you a sandwich?" Detective Winston asked, walking towards the kitchen with Caution and Molly following.

"That would be nice," Caution returned.

"Poof," the detective said, waving her arms around, "You're now a sandwich."

Caution looked at the detective for a second, confused. Then all of a sudden, her eyes crinkled up and she burst out laughing. It was a contagious laugh and Detective Winston began to giggle. That only caused Caution to laugh even harder sending Winston into a full-blown laugh as well. Poor Molly didn't know what to think and began to bark and spin in a circle.

During the commotion, they didn't see the Murphy's come in and stand by the door watching the show. Molly was first to notice them and stopped her act. The dog almost seemed embarrassed. The laughing stopped.

Caution, looking up, saw her father and ran into his open arms. Detective Winston, who was truly embarrassed, cleared her throat and gave a smile at the sweet reunion.

"Oh, Father, are you alright?" Caution asked, seeing the bandage wrapped around his head and dried blood on the front of his shirt.

"Of course," her father reassured her. "This old noggin is as hard as a brick. It will take a lot more than some thugs to put a dent in it."

"I'm glad you're okay," Detective Winston stated. "Is there a suspect? Did you happen to get a look at him?"

"That's probably why I was hit from behind," Mr. Murphy answered. "So that I wouldn't see them." Changing the direction of the conversation, he said, "Thank you, Detective, for watching our little girl. That was extremely kind of you. Now, if you don't mind, I'm going to say goodnight and go upstairs to change," motioning to his blood-stained shirt. "Caution, sweetheart," he said, looking right into Winston's eyes, "why don't you say goodnight to the nice detective and then you can tell me what the two of you have been doing."

Caution looked up at Detective Winston saying, "Thank you for staying with me." She then surprised everyone by running the few yards separating them, giving Winston a big hug. "Please come back to visit."

Mrs. Murphy jumped in quickly, "Yes, thank you so very

much. I don't know what I would have done if you weren't here."

"She's a delight," Winston said, returning the hug. Even Molly went over and leaned against the pair.

"Caution, go with your father up the stairs, he may still be a little wobbly," Mrs. Murphy said. "I'll see the detective out."

Caution went over and took her father's hand, "Good night, Detective," she said, beginning to lead him out of the kitchen.

"Good night," Detective Winston said, with a smile, "and you may call me Vickie." Giving her a wink for good measure.

"Good night, Vickie," Caution said, over her shoulder.

"Let me show you to the door, Detective," Mrs. Murphy said, walking her to the front entrance. "Again, thank you for staying with Caution."

"Mrs. Murphy, did your husband make a report of the mugging?"

"Well, honestly, I don't know," Mrs. Murphy shook her head. "He was at the hospital for a while before I got there. I don't know if he talked to any police officers at the office or at the hospital."

"Did he say anything was taken or did the mugger say anything?"

"Detective, I don't know anything," Mrs. Murphy said,

throwing up her hands. "Why don't you give him a couple days to feel better and ask him," she continued, opening the door for the detective. "For now, I need to attend to him and get Caution in bed."

"Mrs. Murphy, I want to help. I really do," Detective Winston said, taking a step out and then turning. "I don't know if the break-in and tonight's mugging are related or just a coincidence. I don't know what someone could be after. And I sure don't want Caution in the middle of this if there is more to it. Do you?"

"Detective. Vickie," Mrs. Murphy began again, more softly and smiling, yet giving a quick glance behind her, "it's obvious Caution likes you and maybe it's a mistake to let her think we are all good friends now, but let's keep this on a professional level. You have a job to do and Mr. Murphy and I can take care of Caution. Let's leave it at that, shall we?"

"Good night, Mrs. Murphy," Winston said, nodding her head, "I'll get you the report on the burglary and check on the mugging report for you." As she began to walk to her car, she stopped and turned. "Oh, and what was it your husband said? 'The mugger hit him from behind so that he wouldn't see him?'"

"Yes, that's what he said," Mrs. Murphy agreed.

"No, that's not quite right," Winston shook her head, "as I recall, he said it was so that he wouldn't see *'them'*. I believe he was referring to the *'thugs'* he mentioned. And why is the blood on the front of his shirt? Kind of makes you wonder, doesn't it?"

Winston turned, heading once again for her car, leaving Mrs. Murphy standing in the doorway, mouth open.

William N. Gilmore

CHAPTER 19

"They still be there, ain't they?" Big Mike asked in a frightened tone.

"They're still here," Patrick said, as he dug up the cloth holding the coins. "Go and make sure no one is coming."

Mike reluctantly left Patrick's side, going over to the barn door and looking out. "It's clear."

Patrick took out three of the gold coins and retied the corners. He put the cloth bag back in the hole on top of the others, covering them up again and tapping the dirt down with his foot. He went over to the chest, opening the lock with the makeshift key Big Mike fashioned for him, removing one of the money belts from the chest and put the coins in it. He tied the belt around his waist, under his shirt and adjusted his suspenders.

"I think it's supposed to go inside your trousers too," Big Mike suggested. "That way it won't be noticed."

Patrick gave a huff and slipped out of his suspenders again, opening his trousers and then tying the belt to his waist. He put his shirt over the belt, tucking his shirt into his pants and getting back into his suspenders.

"That's better, don't you think?" asked Big Mike. "I can't even tell you have it on."

"There are only three coins in it, eejit," Patrick said, shaking his head. "Of course, you can't tell I have it on. That's the bloody point."

"Well, I wouldn't be able to tell if you placed them in your pocket either," Mike returned. "So, why wear the belt for just three of them?"

"You would soon enough," Patrick said, hands on his hips, "because I have a hole in my bloody pocket."

Mike gave a great laugh. "And here you be, needles and thread galore, and with a hole in your pocket. Your dear, departed tailor would be so ashamed. What do you have in that trunk to sew up that hole in your bloody noggin?"

"The same thing I have to sew up that trap you call a mouth, you big ox," Patrick said.

The two young men stood there face to face, staring at first and then they started making faces at each other. Within a few seconds, they both were laughing out loud.

*

Patrick took the journal from the trunk and began to write the journey he had taken so far. There was a lot to put down just to catch up to this point. He was up half the night writing.

The next morning, Patrick and Mike borrowed a one mule buggy, driving to town atop a dusty and bumpy dirt road. There hadn't been any rain to speak of since the storm. The early morning breeze started the day off just a bit chilly but warmed with the sun's continued rise. The few large clouds passing over gave the air a quick return to the coolness. It reminded them both of home.

"Do you miss it?" Patrick asked, giving a little flick of the reins.

Big Mike knew immediately what he was asking. "Some, the good parts, of course. I miss me pals."

"You mean the gang?" Patrick asked.

"No. Not the whole gang. There were some who were okay, a few that you could count on, but the worst were cutthroats, mean, and extremely dangerous."

"How were you able to leave?" Patrick asked. "I mean, didn't they have rules about getting out, leaving the gang? I'd heard stories."

"You couldn't leave," Mike said, shaking his head. "They'd never let you go. If you tried to leave, they'd come for you. Force you to come back or murder you just to make an example."

"How did you get away? Why?" Patrick continued.

"I was on my own after my parents died," Mike said, with a far-off look. "I tried to live on the streets, but I wasn't doing so good. I was taken in by the gang and given a job. At first, I was just a decoy while others did the stealing, that gave me a place to belong and food for my belly. As part of the gang, I was protected too. That is until one of the lords wanted to use you."

Patrick understood what Mike was saying. He kept silent at the revelation.

"One of the old guys took me in and taught me stuff. I say 'old guys', but he was only a couple years older than I was. Before too long, I was one of the best at stealing. That's how I learned to open stuff."

"I can understand having to steal to live," Patrick sympathized. "Sometimes you have to do things you don't like to be able to survive."

"There was more," Mike said. "Some very terrible things they made you do. Things I don't want to think about now. I just had to leave. Someone who owed me a favor got me on that ship. I thought if I got far enough away, they couldn't come after me."

Patrick let the conversation die and continued to drive the buggy keeping his eyes straight ahead.

CHAPTER 20

Vickie Winston opened the door to her condo and almost fell in, she was that tired. She hit the light switch before closing the door behind her, bolting the three locks on it before throwing her jacket at the chair of the small table in the hallway where she tossed her keys and parked her service weapon.

She kicked her shoes off walking into the kitchen, grabbed a glass and opening the freezer side of her fridge, grabbed a few ice cubes, letting them clink into the glass. She opened a cupboard and pulled out a half-empty pint bottle of twelve-year-old, eighty proof scotch. She poured some of the liquid into the glass and looked at it, then poured some more.

She returned to her living room and fell into her easy chair. Some of the scotch jumped from the glass onto her blouse. She took her index finger, lifting the drops of alcohol off and put them to her lips.

"Can't waste a drop of this," she said out loud to the framed picture of the young, handsome man and the young child he was holding sitting on the table next to her.

*

Winston woke up in her bed. She didn't even remember dragging herself there after getting home. She shook her head and her eyes flew open. She sat up looking at the clock.

"Oh, crap," she let out. It was already past ten a.m. The alarm didn't go off and she was going to be late. She stood up and losing her balance, she fell back onto the bed in a sitting position. She shook her head once more and it came to her; it was Saturday. Although this was her day off, it was the latest she slept in weeks. Her brain and body needed it.

She continued to sit on the bed and put her face in her hands. This time she shook her head and made an unintelligible sound into her palms. This past week had been really grueling, and she put in a lot of hours. The days ran together and just got away from her. The scotch helped her relax almost too much. It had been a long while since she even opened the bottle.

She fell back on her bed, looking up at the ceiling fan, watching the wide, wooden blades go slowly around. Tears welled and flowed from the far corners of her eyes, streaking down almost to her ears before wiping them away and allowing the cool air from the fan to slowly dry her face.

Winston finally got up and went into the kitchen for some water to chase away the dry throat, finding the empty bottle on the counter. "No wonder I couldn't remember anything?" she said to the bottle, shaking her head.

A quick, refreshing, hot shower and a light breakfast were rejuvenating, getting her ready for the rest of the day, although she really didn't have too many plans. She would call the precinct to check on the assault of Mr. Murphy and then go by the cemetery as she did most Saturdays.

William N. Gilmore

CHAPTER 21

The town wasn't all that big, but much bigger than the village they left earlier that day. There were several different shops and stores lining both sides of the dirt thoroughfare that went through the main section of town.

Many houses were springing up and there were a lot of people walking around, children playing, buggies and wagons going back and forth, and it was awfully noisy compared to the farms. There were several other buildings under construction, hammers pounding and men yelling. It looked like the community was well established and growing. It was all incredibly exciting for Patrick and Mike.

The two young men went straight away to one of the big trading stores. Tying the buggies' mule reins to a post out front, they beat and brushed the considerable dust off each other before entering.

Opening the door, a bell overhead rang, announcing their presence. A few customers looked up at the new arrivals then went back to their business. As the newcomers milled about, a man appeared behind a counter.

"Good day, gentlemen, what can I get for you?" the man said, in a deep accent with which they were unfamiliar.

"Good afternoon, sir," Patrick returned. "We were looking for a bank or a store we could do business with."

"Well, you came to the right place, my Irish friends," said the shopkeeper. "We have a bank being built as we speak, and you can wait the couple of months it will take before its doors will open," he laughed, "or, I'd be happy to help you today, if you'd like."

"Before we buy anything, though," Patrick began, "we'd like to exchange some coins."

"The man behind the counter gave the young men a questionable look. "What have you got there, shillings and pence?"

Patrick fumbled with the money belt under his shirt and was able to get it turned and untied without undoing his trousers or suspenders. He removed the three coins from one of the pouches.

"No sir, we have these," Patrick said, holding out his palms with the three gleaming coins.

The shopkeeper's eyes widened as he spied the beautiful coins in Patrick's hand and started to reach for them.

"We were hoping for a fair rate of exchange," Patrick said, pulling his closed hand back.

"We've already been to several places and was hoping you might be the right one to deal with," Big Mike lied. "We don't like being cheated," he added, giving a fierce look.

"No, you won't be cheated here. You can ask any of my customers. I've been here for years. I'm honest and I deal fair with everyone."

Patrick held out his hand again, allowing the man to take one of the coins. The shopkeeper looked closely at the coin and then placed it between his teeth, giving it a quick test. Removing it, he smiled. "I think we can do business, gentlemen."

William N. Gilmore

CHAPTER 22

Vickie Winston stood looking at the large, gleaming white-marble headstone, the deeply carved names, the memorable dates, staring back. For twelve years now, it had been their resting place. Vickie Winston visited them so many times, she knew the names on the markers surrounding them. She never saw fresh flowers on any of them although every now and then she would see artificial ones left by the cemetery workers or flags on the veteran's sites.

Every time she came to visit and walked by on the well maintained, soft grass, she would say something to those who shared the solemn grounds with her husband and child. Not knowing if they might have family or loved ones who came by often, she wanted to make sure they were not forgotten.

"Hey there, Mr. Freeman, lovely day, isn't it? Mrs. Burgess, your spot is looking rather pretty today. Mr. and Mrs. Dawson, you've been here longer than most, I hope you two are enjoying your long rest. Major Foster, next time I come, I have to bring you a new, miniature flag. We can't have Old Glory getting too tattered no matter how small she is. Thank you for your service, sir."

The conversations with her husband and child were more

private. She sat on the grass between them, close enough to touch the headstone. Every now and then, if the day was warm and the grass was dry, she would lie between them.

Sometimes her visits were long, giving her time to talk and tell them what was going on in her life, while other times needed to be cut short because of things she intended to do; like today. Before leaving, she would always place kisses upon the headstone of her loved ones, just above both names. There was an open space for a marker on the other side of her child's. She knew one day they would all be together again. She wiped a tear and walked slowly back to her car.

Winston called the records section of the police department only to find there was not a report made on the assault of Mr. Murphy. She wasn't really sure if she expected there to be one or not. Even though it was her day off, she decided to go to Grady Hospital to check with the ER. They were sure to have the records on Mr. Murphy's treatment including check-in to narrow down the time of the assault.

Why wouldn't he make a report, especially something like an assault? What was he trying to avoid and why? How much did Mrs. Murphy know? She kept asking herself these questions, ones she didn't have any answers to, yet.

*

Winston arrived at the hospital, going into the emergency room entrance past an old, crusty security guard and approached the check-in desk, showing her badge and identification to the admission's attendant.

"I want to get information on a man who came in last night somewhere about seven-thirty with a head injury from an assault. The name's Sean Murphy, white male, about fifty-five."

"Did he come in by ambulance or was he a walk-in?"

"I believe he was a walk-in."

"Was he admitted or just treated in ER?" the attendant asked.

"He was treated and released," Winston said.

The attendant looked through her files and then checked on her computer. She re-checked and then got up, "Just a minute, let me check in another location."

"This isn't happening," Winston said, under her breath.

The attendant returned after just a few minutes, shaking her head, "I'm sorry, detective, we don't have anything for a Murphy last night."

"Do you have anything by any name matching that description last night?" Winston inquired, "Someone who may have paid in cash for treatment?"

"Yes, there was one man last night," the attendant stated, going through her files again. "It's highly unusual for someone to pay full charges in cash and not use insurance. Here it is; a Mr. John Swift. He was signed in at seven-forty-three for an injury to the head. He said he had been mugged and asked us to call his wife."

"Who treated him?" Winston asked.

"Doctor Menzel. Come on around here and look if you'd like."

Winston went around the desk and looked at the small computer screen. The bright white letters on the black background were going by pretty fast. The attendant stopped them at a section with more patient information.

"There were some x-rays taken and a few stitches, but there's not any information about a diagnosis. It doesn't say anything about the time he was released, just that the bill was paid in full with our night accountant."

"When will Doctor Menzel be back on duty?" Winston asked.

"Just a second," the attendant was again on her computer and a new section appeared, "he'll be back tonight. His shift is from six until about two, depending on how busy we are."

"You've been more than helpful. Thank you," said Winston, smiling.

CHAPTER 23

"Four American dollars, each?" Big Mike repeated, shaking his head. "I'm saying five, so why don't we stop this foostering and call it four and a half and we stay friends."

"He's saying you're wasting our time," Patrick told the store owner. "I agree with him," Patrick said, putting the coins back into the money belt. He and Mike began to walk towards the door.

"Okay, okay," the man said, stopping them for the moment. "I'll give you four and a bit."

Patrick and Mike continued to walk and as Patrick grabbed the doorknob, they were stopped once again.

"Four and a half it is," The owner said in a huff. "I'll give you four and a half American dollars each for the coins."

Patrick and Mike stopped and gave a slight glance at each other and smiled before they turned and headed back to the counter.

"That weren't so hard now, was it?" Big Mike asked.

"We're also interested in finding passage to California," Patrick said. "Overland that is," he added, looking at Mike.

The store owner looked at the two men and gave a laugh, "That's a long, hard journey. It could take you four months or more to get there. You're sure not going to do it on thirteen dollars. Sorry, thirteen and a half."

"And just how much do you think it will take? Patrick asked.

"Just the two of you? You'd never make it. If the injun's didn't have your scalps in a couple months, then you might freeze, die from the heat, or a slow death of thirst or disease. Why don't you see about taking a ship around the Horn and keep your hair and your lives?"

"No ships," Big Mike said, not wasting any words or giving an explanation.

"How much?" Patrick asked, once again. "Just the two of us, fully outfitted?"

"I'd say about four or five hundred," the man said, looking carefully at Patrick and Mike for a reaction. "You got that much?"

Patrick didn't answer that question, instead, he asked, "Are there any other wagons going west?"

"Not from here," the owner laughed again. "You need to get to St. Louis or even as far west as Independence before you even think about getting outfitted. And by the time you get there, it will probably cost you a whole lot more. There's a bunch of people headed for California. I was almost one of them. The people who are really going to strike it rich are the ones doing the selling to all the fools headed out there. No offense."

"None taken," Patrick returned. "How do we get to those places?"

"Since we're still friends," the shopkeeper said, with a big grin, "I can tell you everything you need to know, and it won't cost you much for the information."

*

The two dollars they gave the store owner seemed well worth it. Although Big Mike had some idea of where he was going, getting there was a whole new set of problems he was just now finding out about.

Before they could even really get started, they would have to get to Pittsburgh; then by boat on the Ohio River to Missouri. At least this was on a river with land always in sight and not on an ocean. It was a bitter pill that Mike had no choice but to swallow.

They would then pass St. Louis to get to Independence along the Missouri River. This is where they would get outfitted for the overland trek and hopefully team up with other wagons, taking one of the established trails. Possibly the Santa Fe.

Almost halfway along the trail they needed to make a choice; either the Mountain route, that was longer and harder or the Cimarron route that was shorter, had many dangerous river crossings and was known for Indian attacks.

There would be many decisions to be made along the trail. Making the wrong one could delay them for days or weeks, and at worst, get you killed. Disease took most lives along the way. Mishaps; including, getting run over by a wagon, drowning, and accidentally shooting one's self, were at the top as well.

It would not be easy. It would be harder than hard. The body and the spirit would be challenged daily, pushed to and sometimes beyond the breaking point, but if you made it, the rewards just might be worth the hardship and heartache.

As Patrick and Mike left the store, headed for the only hotel in town, Mike put his arm around Patrick's neck, saying, "With your tailor getting drowned and saving my life and all, and with no bloody place to go, I was going to take you to California with me. Now, it looks like you're taking me with you. You have put me in a strange predicament. Now I have to strike it rich just to pay you back."

"But you're forgetting something there, Big Mike," Patrick responded, "It wasn't my money to start with. Suppose I drowned too, whose money would it be?"

"Well, it sure wouldn't be mine," Mike said, throwing up his arms, giving Patrick's neck a rest. "Without you having been there, I'd be cleaning Davy Jones' locker about now."

"What you mean is if Davy had any chests of gold down there, you would have picked them open and would be cleaning them out," Patrick laughed.

Big Mike laughed too. "I'm hungry. You think they have any food at the hotel?"

"Are you buying?" Patrick asked.

"With what, my good looks?" Mike responded.

"Then I guess you'll be going to bed hungry," Patrick said, stone-faced.

Mike stopped in his tracks. "Well, I did help negotiate what you got."

Patrick couldn't hold it any longer and gave a good belly laugh. Big Mike just stared at him for a few seconds, then grabbing Patrick up and tossing him over his shoulder like a big sack of potatoes, he began to run towards the hotel.

Poor Patrick couldn't get a word out and gasped just enough air in to keep from passing out. Several passersby watched wide-eyed as the big man, acting like a schoolboy bully, trotted down the street with his unwilling passenger who was making unintelligible sounds as he barely held onto his hat as he bounced up and down on the massive shoulder of his abductor.

William N. Gilmore

CHAPTER 24

Detective Winston knew her next stop was going to be the Murphy Building. She had no other plans for her day off, so she wanted to see for herself if there might be any evidence still present or if there were any cameras in the area that might have captured the assault.

Every turn brought new questions and few answers. She wasn't sure why she was so interested in this case. Maybe it was the strange, young girl, or maybe it was the apparent deception by the parents, mainly the father. It bothered her. She knew it would continue to bother her until she got answers to all the lingering questions. Sometimes though, answers took you to places you didn't want to go.

Vickie struck out at the Murphy building. There weren't any cameras that could help and there was nothing found that might be evidence. There was too much construction dust, too many retaining walls, and barricades all around. And that's even if the incident actually happened there.

With the Murphy's not willing to be forthcoming, it appeared to be a dead end. Just to be sure though, and to feed her hungry curiosity, Vickie decided she would check once more at the hospital ER later that evening to see if Doctor Menzel could add any additional information. In the meantime, she wanted to do a little research on the Murphy family. She headed off to the downtown branch of the public library not sure what she expected to find.

*

Bill Warner dropped Sam off at his house. Well, it was really Sam's mom's house, Bill's daughter, Jenny. Sam's father took off when he was still a toddler and Bill was glad he was gone. He could tell things were not right for a while between Jenny and What's His Name; he hadn't said his real name out loud for a long time.

When Jenny became more distant to her own father; stopped having him over, phone calls becoming infrequent and short, and the slight cracking of her voice at times when they did talk, Bill became suspicious; not as a detective, but as a father. Dropping in on her unexpectedly one day at the apartment she had then, he saw the fear in her eyes, and the bruises, and then the tears.

As an angry father and grandfather who carries a gun everywhere, every day, he called upon a superhuman effort of restraint at that moment to keep from using it. He was very persuasive when it came to making sure no one would ever hurt his daughter or grandson, or cause them to fear for their safety. If anyone ever did, he would use his considerable talents to ensure no one would ever find the body or pieces of body of the person who had. He made this well-known to What's His Name and apparently, the point was taken to heed.

Bill moved his daughter and grandson into their present house, cutting all ties with What's His Name, having him sign over all parental rights and making sure there would be no legal backlash of any kind. He had the friends and contacts to ensure What's His Name would stay far away and never be heard from again. It was in What's His Name's best interest.

Bill's wife had been gone now for about twelve years. He still lived in the home they shared for the twenty before that. He kept it well maintained, which became one of his main hobbies. The yard along with the garden his wife had started, wasn't. That was one of the homeowner duties he refused to do himself. The mowing, trimming and raking he left to someone else, hiring a company to take care of the yard twice a month.

He often tried to get his daughter and Sam to move in with him, but Jenny liked the schools Sam was going to and her work was real close to her house. Besides, she enjoyed the independence and the freedom without her father looking ever so closely over her shoulder. She still had a life. And Sam came over all the time, sometimes for long weekends, especially when he was out of school, and he was out for only a few more weeks.

Bill was driving down his street, passing a cable company truck going in the opposite direction. He hoped the cable hadn't gone out again in the neighborhood. It was set up to record some of his favorite shows.

Bill pulled into his driveway, parked, and walked out to check the mailbox; nothing, which was strange. He always received at least some kind of junk mail. It's not Sunday or a holiday, he thought, shaking his head. "Oh, well, " he said out loud to himself, "at least no bills. "

He walked back to the front door, getting the right key ready to unlock the deadbolt. He froze. The door was slightly open. His mind did a quick time travel back to when he left that morning. Was it possible he somehow forgot to fully close the door and lock it? He wasn't that old yet. He always locked it.

Bill stood to the side of the door and pushed it open slightly, hesitating just a second before taking a quick peek in. What he saw made him draw his gun, just as he had done in many similar situations while he was with the department.

CHAPTER 25

Pittsburgh was the biggest and the busiest city either of the young men experienced so far in this new land. Wagons, horses, and oxen so thick, it was hard to walk anywhere without having to jump out of the way of something before it ran over or trampled you.

They sold their wagon and team they bought for the trip to Pittsburgh. The small hotel room they were able to get was even smaller with the trunk and other belongings they stashed before going out to explore the city.

The rivers were crowded with ships and boats of every kind. Although Big Mike already made his feelings known about water travel, the two had little choice other than months of open water on the sea route around South America. Patrick explained to Mike the faster they got to California, the quicker they would have gold in their pockets. Big Mike gave in and accepted that they had to travel along the river route; he didn't like it, but he understood. At least they would be in view of land the whole way. The thoughts of all that gold outweighed his fear of drowning, but only by a little.

Along Pittsburgh's Mon Wharf, there must have been forty or fifty stern and side wheelers, and boats of every kind.

After checking on most of them, which were all booked, they finally found what they were looking for; a riverboat that could take them to the jumping off ports in Missouri. Luckily there was still room and although passage was not cheap, they secured a stateroom for both of them. The boat, almost 300 feet long was leaving in just two days.

They were able to stay on the boat until sailing for just a bit more although Big Mike whined about that. He really hated the water now. But it was cheaper than the hotels and probably safer, if the boilers didn't explode. Mike was eager to get out and have a look around the large city, but Patrick didn't want to chance getting robbed or taken advantage.

He exchanged many of the gold coins but kept most in reserve. He tried to budget and be frugal with the money not knowing what kind of prices they would run into when it came time to outfit for the overland journey. Everything was priced high and getting higher every day.

He was writing out a list of items when Mike entered the cabin.

"Come on, Patrick, me lad." Mike was pleading, "We have to see what's out there. It be mighty exciting. I can't remember seeing so many people and so many bloody shops. There must be twenty saloons, not two minutes from here."

"That's just exactly why I'm staying here. I have to watch over our belongings and keep our money safe. If something were to happen to it, then what would we do? We wouldn't have a pot to piss in and there would be no grand adventure, no gold, and no castle overlooking the ocean. No, I'll not be tempted."

Mike gave Patrick his sad, dejected look. The one he had worked on for weeks. He slowly hung his head and shifted his weight from foot to foot, wringing his cap in his hands.

"We will be needing provisions for the trip and I'm getting mighty hungry," Patrick proclaimed. "One of us needs to go, and it won't be me."

Mike dared to look up with one eye and saw Patrick with a smile as he held out his hand with a number of silver dollars.

"One beer. Just one, and then you get what we need."

The big man straightened up, took a few steps forward and reached out for the large coins, but Patrick pulled them back at the last second, startling Mike.

"You will agree and promise that after your one beer, you will get the things I put on this list. You will come straight back here and not dilly-dally around. One beer, no gambling, no women, and no fights. Just the bloody things on the list, is that clear?"

"Yes, Mother," Mike said.

"Don't talk to anyone," Patrick said as he placed the coins in Mike's hand along with a piece of paper. "Here's a list of things we need for now. Find a shop that is fair. Make a good bargain. Don't let them take you. Get just the things on the list."

"How can I bargain with them if I can't talk with them?" Mike used his famous logic.

"That's the only people you can talk with," Patrick said.

"How will the bartender know what I want if I can't tell him?" Mike asked, showing just the hint of a smile.

Patrick picked up a shoe and threw it at Mike, somehow missing him. Mike quickly went out the door as Patrick also threw a barrage of curses at him.

After Mike left, he took out the journal and began to write, catching up on all the events and included descriptions of the places and people they had seen or met.

One day, when I'm old, he thought to himself, *I'll read this and look back on what my life was about or read it to my own son or daughter when they ask me what I did when I was young. I guess I better not tell too big of a lie.*

CHAPTER 26

Bill scanned his house through the open back door. It had been ransacked. Not knowing if whoever had done this was still inside, he backed off and called for a patrol unit. If someone was still there, there was no need to go in alone, even if he was armed.

Without the use of their sirens as Bill had requested, two patrol units arrived, one who was an old friend of Bill's. One officer remained at the front of the house, while Bill and the other officer entered the house from the back door, weapons at the ready. They began to check the house for an intruder. Room by room, checking every door and possible hiding place, the house was cleared. Someone had made a mess of several rooms, including Bill's bedroom and den.

Nothing seemed to be missing. His computer was still there along with his television and other electronics. A large clear bottle with cash and coins had not been disturbed. It seemed as if someone had been looking for something in particular. The other officer was radioed to come around and stated the front and sides were secure and still locked with no windows broken or open.

"What's going on here, Bill?" Sergeant Kevin Arant, an

eighteen-year veteran asked. "You have a burglary with nothing taken."

"Maybe I scared them off. I'll have to do an inventory and check. Someone was after something," Bill said.

"There's no forced entry. A mad ex-girlfriend maybe or someone else who has a key?" the sergeant asked.

"No exes and just my daughter has a key," Bill explained.

"Okay, you want me to have a CSI team come give it a once over?"

"No, I don't need all the people here and that powder thrown around the house. It's going to be enough just to clean up this mess. I'll just make a report to document it. I may need it for insurance if something does come up missing. Have there been any other burglaries in the area recently?"

"Actually, no. It's been very quiet around here. This has always been one of the better areas we have in the zone, but that's why you live here. We'll add some patrols anyway. We don't need to let this stuff get started here."

"Okay, Kevin. Thanks."

Bill had a mess to clean up. Whoever had been in his house made sure of that. Turned over furniture, broken lamps, drawers emptied, clothes tossed around. It was if they were there just to make a mess, not take anything. But this wasn't just an ordinary burglary and Bill wasn't just an ordinary victim.

Although Bill was retired from the department, all those

years of experience hadn't just gotten up and left. He got back into police mode and looked at the situation. No forced entry. He went to the back door and took a look at the lock with a magnifying glass. There were some scratches and a bit of gray powder in the keyhole. It was graphite powder to help the lock turn easily. The lock had been picked.

He got his own fingerprint kit which he still had and checked the door and lock area. Nothing. He knew there would not be any fingerprints. Gloves may have been worn, but that would be after the lock was picked for sensitivity. Then it was wiped down taking all the prints off, even his own.

Nothing of value was taken. Not even items in plain sight like the jar of money or the electronics. This was not some homeless person or junkie, nor even a neighborhood kid looking for a thrill or money to buy his next video game. This was someone who had experience; someone on a mission. That made it even more disturbing.

While Bill was evaluating the situation, a knock came at his front door. He went and found it was his elderly, next-door neighbor, Mrs. Jenkins. She would often come over to talk after Bill's wife had passed away or to bring him a pie or cake she had made. Pushing eighty, she still got around pretty well and kept herself active.

"Hey, Mrs. Jenkins. I'm sorry, but I'm a little busy right now," he made the excuse. He didn't want to scare or worry her with information on the burglary.

"I see you had some friends over earlier. Nice. I still love men in uniforms. My Jonathan was in the army for twenty-two years, you know. Anyway, I was wondering if you were still having problems with your cable?"

"My cable? I don't know."

"I saw the cable man pull into your driveway and hoped he wouldn't mess up my soap operas."

"You saw the cable guy at my house? When was this?"

"About an hour before you got home. I think you just missed him."

Bill recalled passing a cable company van on his street. *Could that have been my burglar?* He wondered.

"I'll come back later when you are not so busy," Mrs. Jenkins said and started to turn.

"Oh, no. You're not bothering me at all," Bill hurriedly said. "Tell me more about this cable guy," he said with a smile. He guided her to one of the chairs on the front porch. "Did you get a good look at him?"

"Well, of course, I did. He was wearing a uniform. Did I tell you my Jonathan was in the army for twenty-five years? He was handsome in his uniform."

"Yes ma'am, I'm sure he was. About the cable guy, what else did you happen to see? Was he tall or short? Fat or slim?"

"He was wearing a blue uniform. It was very nice. He was tall, about your age and he had a toolbox as I recall. He went around to the back of your driveway. Was he able to fix your cable?"

"I believe he did," Bill said. "Did he have any facial hair or other characteristics you may have seen?"

"You shouldn't have a beard while in uniform," she said, sternly. "My Jonathan never did. Not while he was in the army all those twenty-seven years."

"No, ma'am. Did he happen to see you, the cable guy?"

"Oh, no, dearie, I was looking—well, I just happened to be dusting my blinds at the time. I heard the van and was hoping it was my Jonathan coming home. You know he was in the army? He's coming home soon."

"Thank you, Mrs. Jenkins. You've been very helpful," Bill said as he stood, holding his hand out to help the old lady up from the chair. "I've got to get back to my cleaning now. I hope you have a nice day."

"After Jonathan gets home," the pleasant elderly lady said, "we'll have you and your wife over for dinner one night."

"That would be delightful," Bill said, with a sad smile.

As his elderly neighbor slowly walked back to her property, Bill couldn't help but feel sorry for her. In her advanced age, Alzheimer's apparently had set in along with her other problems.

Shortly after they were married, and with her pregnant, her husband, an army private, had been shipped overseas during WWII. While in Germany near the end of the war, after several days of a heavy back and forth battle, he was listed as missing in action. He was never found. Her daughter told him the story and how her mother never gave up hope that one day he would come home. She still believed it. She still waited for her Jonathan in his nice army uniform.

*

"You didn't tell me this guy was a cop," the voice said.

"I didn't know," Tom Dearing said into the phone, a bit surprised. "Did you find it?"

"No, and I ain't goin' back lookin' again either. Too dangerous. It could be anywhere."

"Did anyone see you?"

"Nah. Wouldn't matter if they did. I went in disguised as a cable guy. Even grabbed one of their trucks just to make it look good. Walked right up to the front door and knocked. No one home so I went in the back door. Nice, neat place, or at least it was. I dumped the truck and torched it when I was done."

"Did you look in the kid's room?"

"Ain't no kids room. Don't think he lives there. Pictures all over of an older lady and some of a kid and a younger lady, his mom I guess. Guy must be the grandfather."

"Yeah, that's what I figured at the shop. Any clues to

where the kid lives?"

"Naw, but if the guys a cop, I'd back off. Especially now that I've trashed his house and he knows someone's looking for something. Like I said, a little too dangerous right now."

"I hear you," Tom stated, "but this could be the big one." He hesitated for a moment. "Okay, let's play it safe. Lay low for a while."

"Maybe you should follow your own advice."

"I'll think about it. Stay close to a phone; I'll be in touch."

William N. Gilmore

CHAPTER 27

Big Mike found himself in the Pittsburgh crowd of people who were trying to get somewhere other than where they were. The many carts and wagons stirred up the muddy ways while the street hawkers tried to sell their wares or get a handout.

There was one fellow who stood out and was drawing a crowd, yelling and waving his fists, complaining about the corruption in the city; surely a preacher or a politician.

The city police arrived and after several attempts to get him to stop, they arrested him, but not without some members of the crowd with conflicting views getting into their own fight.

"Who is that?" Mike asked one of the bystanders.

"That's Joseph Barker," the man said. "He's a street preacher, but he's rebelling against all the corruption the present mayor and all the local politicians are involved in. If I have anything to say about it, he'll be our next mayor."

The fights subsided and most of the onlookers soon went about their own business.

Mike wasn't sure which way to go himself, that is, until he saw one of the many overhead signs for a saloon.

One beer. That's what Patrick had said. One. And he found the perfect place to get it too. 'O'Mally's Saloon' the sign read. What could be better than to visit a place where his countrymen might be, where he could get a real Irish beer, where he would feel at home, and maybe even get some directions to the shops he would need later?

Mike made his way across the muddy street and into the crowded, smoky establishment. A few heads turned his way, some of the conversations ceased, and a few tankards were lowered as the big man made his way to the bar.

"What will it be?" The man behind the bar asked.

Mike ordered his one beer.

Behind the bar and high on the wall was a large green flag with a golden harp in the center. The figure of a busty winged woman, the Maid of Erin, made up the front of the harp.

Lifting his mug to the flag, "God bless Ireland," Mike said, with his deep brogue; more than a few repeated it back, lifting their glasses high. He took a big slug of the cool beer, giving a huge sigh and wiping the foam from his mouth with his sleeve. Things went quickly back to normal. Well, almost.

A young man, maybe a few years older, but not nearly as big as Mike, sat at a back table, his back to the wall. He had a big cigar sticking out of his mouth and a well-worn, black derby sitting on his head. He always watched who came into the bar, but this time, he paid special attention to Mike when he entered, made his way to the bar, and ordered a beer from the barkeep.

He looked Mike over, up and down. That large muscular

build and the face with the big grin was unmistakable; unforgettable.

The man at the table got up and as soon as he did, others moved out of his way and made a path as if it were the Red Sea parting again. He slowly made his way through a thick haze of blue-gray smoke towards the bar. Mike had his back to the man and didn't see him approach, nor did he see the man reach inside the right side of his jacket and grab the long handle sticking from his belt.

All the conversations died at that moment and Mike noticed the wide-eyed stares. He slowly turned to face a man with a very large knife in his extended left hand. The man was holding the nasty point of that deadly, sharp knife right under Mike's chin, directed straight at his Adam's apple.

William N. Gilmore

CHAPTER 28

Detective Winston returned to Grady Hospital and made her way slowly through the Emergency Room looking for Doctor Menzel. She had been directed by a nurse to where he might be found. Given a description of the man, she saw the doctor at a station writing in a notebook.

"Doctor Menzel?" Winston inquired.

"Yes, may I help you?"

I'm Detective Winston," the policewoman stated, showing her badge and ID. "I'm investigating the assault of a man you may have treated last night. He gave his name as John Swift and he had a head injury."

"Yes, I remember him. Very quiet. Didn't say much about the incident. Didn't want to call the police about it."

"Did the injuries appear to have been made from behind or from the front," Winston asked.

"The wounds were from something that may have been metal, not a pipe, however, or other cylindrical object. They appeared to have been delivered while Mr. Swift was facing the person.

"Could the object have been a handgun?"

"I believe so. I've seen many wounds of that nature and

these were consistent with a pistol whipping. He needed a few stitches and his head bandaged. X-rays were taken and were clear. I don't believe there was a concussion."

"Was there anything else that seemed strange or suspicious to you?"

"A woman arrived later, his wife I presume, she was very upset. I recall he told her not to talk with anyone or say anything. I learned later he paid cash for the treatment, which was highly unusual, and sometime after that, they left."

"So, there was never any police called and no report made while they were here?"

"Not that I saw. If it were me, I'd be screaming bloody murder. I'd want the suckers caught and strung up."

"I think most people would," Winston said, "at least, those who didn't have something to hide. Thanks for your time, doctor."

*

Bill Warner called his friend, Sergeant Arant and gave him the information about the cable truck and the sketchy description of the 'cable guy'. Kevin said he would check reports and have his patrols keep their eyes out and get back to him.

The coin was the only thing new and there were already many questions around it, not the least of which was the break-in and then there was Tom Dearing.

Bill checked the phone book and found several coin shops that had been in business for a long time and had a Better

Business stamp of approval. He found one matching his criteria and called. Speaking with the owner, and without telling him what he had, he learned what Dearing had told him was pretty much true. There were not any British gold sovereigns known to be minted in 1840, however, there were rumors and stories that popped up from time to time about conspiracies, royal intrigue, pirates, and of course, treasure.

The dealer also told him of a big coin show and sale that was being held this weekend at one of the local hotel conference centers and invited him to attend. Bill told him he would think about it and appreciated the information.

William N. Gilmore

CHAPTER 29

Mike's eyes were focused too much on the knife to see the man clearly. It wasn't until the man spoke that Mike's eyes showed any fear.

"So, ye thinks ye could run away and hide yerself here in this big, bloody country, now do ye?" The man asked.

Mike looked down, past the knife and as the thick brim of the hat rose, into the menacing eyes of the man. It was 'Jimmy the Blade' Dugan, a lord of his former gang, the Ormond Boys.

"Ye better enjoy that cool beer, boy," Jimmy said, with a twisted smile, "cause it could be the last one ye ever taste."

Mike stared into those eyes for what seemed an eternity, waiting for the knife to slice deep into his throat when he saw the man's stern face crack just a bit. Just a few seconds longer and the man couldn't hold it any longer. He let out a big belly laugh, took the knife and stabbed it into the bar top, then grabbed Mike giving him a huge bear hug, causing him to spill most of his beer. Everyone in the bar let out a big sigh and then joined in the laughter.

"This be my mate from home," Jimmy announced to the entire room. "This here be Mikey the Mountain," slapping Mike on the back. "He be one of us, an Ormond Boy."

Jimmy retrieved his knife from the bar, sticking it back into his belt. He locked his arm in Mike's and ushered him over to his table. He told one of the girls to bring Mike a fresh beer, on the house.

"Just what the bloody hell are ye doin' here, Mikey? Are ye alone? Are any of the other Boys here with ye?"

"I'm on my way to California. No one came with me from the gang. I'm going for the gold," Mike stated the truth, but not offering all of it.

Jimmy let out another big laugh. "That's why I came too, that and the bloody Royal Irish Constabulary, but I found my gold right here. I own this saloon and two others."

A pretty, red-headed saloon girl put a fresh beer down in front of Mike and gave him a big smile and a wink.

"I own them too," Jimmy said, swatting the girl on the rear as she turned. She jumped and gave a little squeal.

"But the sign says 'O'Mally's Saloon'?"

"He was the owner before me and we became partners, but the partnership was dissolved," Jimmy smiled, patting the handle of his knife. "I just haven't changed the bloody sign yet. I might just keep it that ways in his remembrance. He was a good Irish Catholic after all."

"Are there others here from the Boys?" Mike asked, scared someone might have brought the truth about his departure with them.

"Only a handful; Fingers Finney (one of the smoothest pickpockets south of Dublin), Morey the Mouth; he's over there telling some of his wild stories, and Danny the Duck (so named because of a bad leg that made him waddle when he walked), came over with me. A few others came shortly after, but we be growing, and we may start something even better over here, and I want ye to be part of it."

"Sounds grand, but I already have plans. I'm going straight away to California. I'm just passing through."

"Now, don't make up ye bloody mind so fast. Ye pot o' gold might just be right here," Jimmy stated, pointing his finger at the floor. "It's a long, dangerous journey. Things could happen." Jimmy's face showed he wasn't ready for a refusal.

"Yeah, I'll give it some thought," Mike said. He already had and knew it would be safer with Patrick on the trail than it ever would be with Jimmy in Pittsburgh.

Jimmy raised his own mug high and cried out, "The Ormond Boys."

Everyone in the bar raised their drinks and repeated the cheer, "Ormond Boys", including Mike.

Mike knew he had to get out of there; and soon. He didn't need any more questions asked of him and he wasn't about to tell them about Patrick or the boat they would be on. He didn't want to draw suspicion on himself leaving so soon, but Patrick may start to get worried and come looking for him if he was too late returning to the boat and he sure didn't want him to find him with 'Jimmy the Blade' of the Ormond Boys. He had to come up with a plan in a hurry.

CHAPTER 30

After a few hours, Sergeant Arant called Bill back with some information.

"One of the cable company's trucks was stolen this morning," Kevin told him. "It was found burning in a field this afternoon about the same time you made your report. It was found by one of the patrols before the stolen report had even been made. Total loss, no evidence. Could be your burglar, but there's no way to tell."

"It's him," Bill said. "Cable trucks don't scream out joy ride and why torch it? It's him," he said, again.

"Just let me know if there is anything else I can check for you," the sergeant said.

"Thanks, Kevin, I will."

Bill Warner had a long night of cleaning and placing unbroken items back where they belonged. His house now looked close to normal.

Bill had also gone to the local home improvement store and bought a security system that included door alarms and video cameras for the front and rear of the house. It only took several hours to install, but it would give him a huge peace of mind. Unfortunately, it would not be enough for him to want Sam to come over to the house for a while. His grandson's safety was his main priority.

*

In the morning, Sean Murphy made his way downstairs and was on the way to his study, trying hard not to be noticed by his wife, but as intuitive as wives can be, he wasn't very successful.

"What are you doing out of bed?" His wife asked.

"I'm just going to the study. Thought I'd do a little research for my book. I'm getting bored up there and besides, I'm feeling much better. There's no dizziness and not much pain anymore. I'm fine."

"Right," she said sarcastically. "Until you fall on your face or have a blood clot give you a stroke at your desk."

"That could happen in bed."

"What, falling on your face?"

They both laughed at that.

"Really, I'm fine," he insisted. "If I thought otherwise, I wouldn't have gotten up or I would have stayed at the hospital."

"It's your head," she said grudgingly. "I'm just glad I have a lot of insurance on you," she snickered. "Can I get you some breakfast or at least some coffee?"

"That would be lovely. Where's Caution?"

"She's outside with Molly. They've gotten very close in such a short time. I think bringing her home was one of your best ideas. She gets outside more, she's more responsible, and I can tell that Molly would protect her from just about anything."

"Just as we hoped," he said."

Sean went into his study, closed the door and went to a section of the bookcase on the wall. He reached for a book, *Gulliver's Travels,* and tilted it back. There was a 'click' and part of the bookcase popped open just a bit. Behind the section of bookcase was a long, deep safe. He spun the combination dial several times, operating it through a series of numbers. After the last one, he twisted the handle that opened the safe.

Inside the safe on a shelf was some cash, a book of documents including wills, passports, pictures, personal items, and a leather-bound journal. A wooden presentation box containing a Colt Peacemaker was on another shelf.

Standing up in the corner of the safe was an antique rifle and several map cases containing some very old maps. He took the maps out placing them on a table. After removing them from the cases, he carefully unrolled one that had the northern U. S. east coast outline and part of the Atlantic Ocean. The map was hand-drawn, ink on parchment, without any other color.

He placed paperweights at both ends of the map to hold it open. He opened another map with the same shoreline, placing it just above the other map. It was obvious the maps had been drawn by two different people, yet they were almost identical with very minor differences.

The first map was dated 1850. The second map was dated 1840. Both maps had an 'X' mark that had been placed just off the shoreline and into the Atlantic Ocean.

Sean believed that the 'X' marked where a ship had gone down. No other information was on the maps; no other dates other than the year, no ship names, not even who had drawn the maps.

One ship had been documented only at the time of its sinking in 1850. That's the one his great-grandfather, Patrick Murphy, traveled on from Ireland.

Sean's father had acquired the 1840 map from a map dealer after telling him the story of his grandfather, Patrick, and how he was just trying to establish the location of his entry to the country. The dealer, unaware of the true significance of the map sold it at a bargain price.

Through his own research of family letters, journals, and stories handed down through the ages, Sean came to believe there was much more involved with the location on the maps than just one shipwreck.

Although there were no official records, no first-hand accounts, no known survivors, no witnesses, or any other records or documents to establish a ship had gone down in the same location a decade earlier, Sean was more than convinced one had done so. He had a little inside information.

Sean went back to the open safe and removed a small

wooden box. He removed from it a clear-plastic case containing a brilliant, gold coin. He looked at it closely and smiled. He admired the crown-topped coat of arms; its beauty, the elegance of its design, and the power of its sovereign message.

He turned the coin over, looking at the silhouette of the young and beautiful face of Queen Victoria. She seemed to have a slight smile as if she held a secret. The date below her stood out strong; 1840. Perhaps she held a secret after all.

CHAPTER 31

Mike knew he had to get away from Jimmy and the rest of the transplanted Ormond Boys, get the supplies that he and Patrick needed, and get back to the boat without arousing suspicion. How, was the big question.

"Hey, darlin', bring another round fer meself and me old chum here," Jimmy called out to one of his girls.

"Thanks," Mike said, "but I've got to go and meet a man about some business. How 'bout I come back a little later and we can talk about your offer?"

"It ain't no offer," Jimmy insisted, "it be what we do fer each other; lookin' out fer family. Ye go handle yer bitness and then we can celebrate right. Get all the Boys together and show 'em who we be in this bloody town.

Mike got up, shook hands with Jimmy and started out of the saloon.

"I'll see ye in a wee bit," Jimmy said, holding up his tankard. "Don't make it too late, now laddie, where's I gots to come alookin' fer ye."

Mike looked back, gave a wave, forced a smile, and hurried his pace a little. He was scared to turn his back again, expecting that big knife to strike any moment.

Mike made it outside, wiped his brow, and gave a big sigh of relief. He needed to find a store to get the supplies, not one too close, but far enough away from Jimmy, and then get back to Patrick before he began to worry too much.

As soon as Mike left the saloon, Jimmy made eye contact with one of his Boys. Jimmy gave a nod and the obedient minion bounded for the door.

Patrick was already worried. He paced the small room with thoughts that Big Mike was playing cards, or throwing dice, possibly even with a girl or two, and drinking their money away. He knew he was the one who should have gone. Not that he didn't trust Big Mike, but it may not have been wise to throw him into all that temptation.

He'd give him a while longer before going on a search for him. Something he wouldn't be comfortable with. He didn't dare leave all their belongings out nor the money hidden in the cabin and carrying that much wasn't the wisest thing to do. Besides, he didn't like crowds of people and Pittsburgh was a big town with lots of places to hide; lose yourself or get yourself into a heap of trouble. Of course, when looking for Big Mike the first place to look would be the saloons, the next would be the jail.

CHAPTER 32

Vickie returned to her apartment, but not before stopping at the store to pick up some much-needed groceries and a short side-trip to the liquor store to replace the bottle of scotch she emptied the night before, and a bottle of red wine. Not that she was planning a repeat of the previous evening, but she was still on her weekend off.

Instead of making something quick, she had decided to make a full meal; spaghetti with meat sauce, a salad, French bread with garlic butter, and a nice glass or two of a Merlot wine.

Although she was cooking for one, she often cooked large meals that would provide left-overs for several days. She used to do this for her husband and daughter for the times she had to work late cases and wouldn't get home in time for dinner. Spaghetti used to be one of their favorites.

She loved cooking for her family when she could. Her husband wasn't very good at cooking and would get fast food, order out, or easy-to-heat meals too many times and Vickie would get on to him for allowing their daughter to have junk meals.

She glanced over at the picture of them on the table in the living room and smiled. As she did, the lamp on the table came on, startling her.

"What the hell?" She asked, looking around the room as if expecting to see someone there. She slowly walked into the living room, looking around still. Nothing.

Vickie slowly reached up and to the wheel that turned the light on and off. She turned the wheel and the light went out. She turned it several more times, turning the light on and off several times. She reached up and tested the bulb to make sure it wasn't too hot and twisted the bulb. It moved slightly, tightening into the socket.

"Just a loose bulb, you idiot," Vickie said to herself out loud. "You just thought it was off." She went back into the kitchen but took several glancing looks at the light.

*

Bill Warner and his grandson, Sam, entered the hotel's conference center where the coin show was being held. There must have been a hundred dealers with tables and showcases galore and three times as many patrons.

"Wow!" Sam exclaimed, his eyes opened as wide as they could get.

"Pretty impressive," Bill said. "Now remember," looking down at Sam, "We don't give any information away about the coin, where it was found, nothing."

"I got it, Grandpa," Sam said, smiling. "It's our secret."

"That's right, and we don't want anyone knowing that

we're detectives. We're still undercover."

Sam gave his grandfather a 'thumbs up' and included a wink for good measure.

"Let's go look around. Maybe we can find something for your mother's birthday."

"Okay, but I don't think she likes stuff like this."

"Well, maybe not as something to collect, but when you get a little older, you'll find out just how much women like gold and silver and all things involving money."

"I like money, Grandpa," Sam said, with an even bigger smile.

"Me too," Bill said, nodding quickly. They both laughed. "In fact, I don't know anyone who doesn't."

Bill and Sam walked around for about a half hour, looking at different displays and cases of coins and currency, books, supplies, and everything involving the hobby. They had only seen about a tenth of the dealer's setups.

They came upon the booth of the Atlanta coin dealer Bill had called after he and Sam met with Dearing. Bill introduced himself, shaking hands with Bryan White while Sam ogled over all the coins in a display case.

"I'm hoping to find someone familiar with British Sovereigns and possible shipwreck treasures," Bill explained, keeping his voice as low as possible in the noise of the large crowd.

"Well, the best authority I know would be John Gray.

He happens to have a booth over on the next aisle. He's brought up some of the best and most historic finds this side of the Atocha.

"What's an Ato—" Sam was trying to ask.

"The Atocha," Bryan repeated. "That's a Spanish treasure ship that sank in 1622 near the Florida Keys. It was carrying millions of dollars in gold and silver coins and bars. It was found in July of 1985 by Mel Fisher."

"Mel Fisher," Bill acknowledged, "that's the metal detector guy."

"Yes, among many more things," Bryan stated. "He's a legend in the treasure hunting world, as well as in metal detectors."

"And this John Gray?" Bill was asking.

"He's your local man if you're looking for information on a certain shipwreck or lost-at-sea treasure. And, he's discreet."

"What do you know about a dealer named Tom Dearing with Quality Coins and Stamps?"

"He's fairly new on the circuit, but he's not someone I would trust. He rubs me the wrong way. I don't think he's really interested with the fun and pleasure of collecting. I think he's into the profit he can make. He over-grades coins he sells, and I think his scales are tilted his way for buying precious metals.

He won't even show his face at the shows, but that's alright with me. I don't think he's good for the hobby."

"Thanks," Bill said. "We'll go and talk with Mr. Gray." They shook hands again and Bill had to almost drag Sam away from the displays.

The next aisle over was a large booth with several tables and large glass displays. Inside one of the larger glass cases were items recovered from shipwrecks. There were flintlock pistols, swords, cannonballs, tankards, pewter plates, and eating utensils; there was even a blunderbuss.

Scattered around the items were gold and silver coins, bars of gold, and links of gold chains. There were rings and necklaces with colored jewels; bright green emeralds, blood red rubies, pearls, and others.

Sam was mesmerized, mostly with the things he associated with pirates. The guns, a treasure chest with gold and silver doubloons, and a long cutlass sword.

"You like pirates?" a voice from behind the case asked.

"Oh, yes," Sam said, without looking away from the display.

"What ten-year-old doesn't?" Bill asked.

"Hi, I'm John Gray," the man introduced himself.

"Bill Warner, and this is my grandson, Sam. Uh, Sam."

"Oh, sorry. Hi," Sam said, finally looking up from all the wonderful items, but only for a second.

Bill smiled. "He's a little overwhelmed."

"I was too the first time I saw it. I'm glad he likes it. It's only a small part of what I've recovered and even everything I've found would not even make a small dent on what remains hidden under all the waters of the world."

"I bet," Bill said, now doing his own staring at the treasures.

"Is there something I can interest you in? It's all for sale."

"I think Mom would like that gold chain," Sam offered.

"I'm sure she would," Grandpa Bill returned.

"It's a bargain today. I have a special show price just this weekend," John said. "It's only two hundred and thirty-five thousand."

"Dollars?" Bill asked, shocked.

"Of course," John replied. "It came from a 1690 shipwreck in the Gulf of Mexico; it's 23 karats; two and a half feet long, and just over four pounds

"I think I'll pass today, but thanks anyway," Bill said.

John laughed. "No problem. Maybe next time."

Bill looked around to see if anyone was within earshot. "What do you know about shipwrecks along the northern east coast in or around 1840?" Bill asked.

"What's the ship's name," John inquired.

"I don't have one. I don't even know where it may have sailed from, or where it was going."

"Do you have a date or at least a month of the sailing or wreck?"

"Only that it may have sunk sometime in 1840 or after," Bill answered.

"That's not a whole lot of information to go on and too much time and ocean to even take a guess. There's nothing that comes to mind," John said, shaking his head. "It would take some very specific research. However, I'm going to be very busy the next couple of months."

Bill thought for a moment and looked down at Sam. He looked back at Gray. "To tell the truth, I'm not really sure if there was a ship. You see, there was something found that makes me believe there may have been a ship, possibly from England. I understand you are someone who can be very discreet."

Now, John looked Bill in the eyes. "I know when to keep my mouth shut if that's what you mean."

Bill reached into his pants pocket and removed the plastic holder, looked around once more, and handed it to the treasure hunter.

John looked at the gold coin and in an instant, his eyes were bigger than Sam's. "Ah, may I ask where you acquired this?" he asked, barely able to get it out.

Bill looked proudly at Sam and placed his hand on the young boy's head. "I just happen to have my own little treasure hunter."

William N. Gilmore

CHAPTER 33

Mike hurried through the crowded streets of Pittsburgh to an area where there were more shops than bars. He found a dry goods store to get most items on the list and then one named Horne's, a new department store where he could get the rest of the items. It took only thirty minutes to find the items, pay for them, and get them packaged up.

The owner, Joseph Horne offered to deliver the goods that afternoon or at least call for a wagon to help him transport the heavy burden, but Mike insisted he could carry everything. Time was not his friend just then.

Mike exited the store with a pair of inquisitive eyes watching his every move from across the street. He had been followed with great stealth, the young man taking every mental note to report back to his boss, Jimmy.

As Mike toted the large bundle over his shoulder back towards the boat and Patrick, Mike believed something was amiss. He felt it more than anything and his feelings were something he paid attention to when they came knocking.

Mike continued until he came upon an alleyway. He made a turn into the alley, and quickly put the package down, flattening himself, as much as he could, against the building.

Within a few seconds, a young lad came around the corner and was startled to see Mike standing there. He froze.

Mike grabbed the kid, pulling him further into the alley and threw him up against the other building so that his brogans dangled several feet off the ground.

"Why are you bloody following me?"

The kid, maybe all of fourteen, short and scrawny with eyes as big as saucers, tried to lie his way out of his predicament.

"I'm sorry, sir, I'm just trying to make my way home. I didn't even know you was here."

"You've been following me for a while. Did Jimmy send you?"

"I don't know what you mean, sir." The boy was looking side to side, maybe to find an escape. "I just want to go home, sir." And then he started to cry.

"This is exactly what they taught us to do back in Dublin if we got pinched. You go back and tell Jimmy I don't need a baby to babysit me. If he wants to know what I'm doing, come and ask me himself. I ain't one of his Boys and it's none of his bloody business."

"He won't like that," the boy said, changing his tune. "Once an Ormond Boy, always an Ormond Boy," the lad said as if he were in a trance.

Mike lowered the boy till he was flat on the ground. Pushed him along and then gave him a kick in the seat of the pants for good measure. "Go back to the safety of your flock, laddie, and tell your bloody shepherd he should keep a rope on you. Tell him if he comes looking, the only thing he just might find is that big knife of his stuck up his arse. Good day to you."

The boy ran off, looking back only once while rubbing his backside. Mike picked up the bag of goods once again and trekked onwards to the boat. He arrived just as Patrick was preparing to start a one-man search party.

"Where have you been?" Patrick asked, "Let me smell your breath."

"Only beer," Mike said. One, okay maybe two, but I only paid for one." He realized he had just said too much.

"And who would be so nice as to spot you a beer?" Patrick inquired.

Mike hesitated for a bit. "I happened upon an old chum from home in a saloon. He was kind enough to buy me a beer. For old time's sake."

Patrick looked Mike up and down and let the interrogation drop. "Did you get everything?" Patrick asked.

"Yes, yes, it be all here," Mike said, a very slight quiver in his speech.

"Are you alright? You seem out of sorts." Mike noticed.

"I got a little lost," Mike lied. "I'm fine now."

"I'm sure that would be easy to do. Let's eat."

"Go ahead, I'm not that hungry."

"Now I know something is wrong. Even if you ate something earlier, I know you wouldn't turn down food now."

Mike grudgingly told Patrick everything, starting with how he came to be alone and having to try and live on the streets of Dublin; being forced into becoming a member of the Ormond Boys; the mistreatment by the lords of the gang until he grew and became feared for his size, and getting away from the gang while back in Ireland, getting on the ship for America.

He got to where he went to the saloon and came across Jimmy 'The Blade'; Jimmy's offer, up to the kid following him through the streets of Pittsburgh. Maybe spending a little too much time describing Jimmy's saloon girls.

Patrick took it all in, keeping quiet while Mike told his story. He knew Mike had been in a gang, but he didn't know it had been the Ormond Boys. He jerked and shuddered to hear the name. Someone from the Ormond Boys killed his brother, someone with a big knife.

"Tell me more about this Jimmy 'The Blade'," Patrick said, slowly.

CHAPTER 34

John Gray had only seen one other coin like the one Bill Warner showed him. John's father, also a diver and collector, had it in his private collection for many years until one day, a man made him an offer too good to refuse.

John hated to see the coin go. He believed it was the most beautiful thing he had ever seen. He was sure there were things in his father's collection that were more valuable and had more meaning, but economic times sometimes caused you to do things you regret.

The location of the coin's recovery, the story behind it, was never revealed to John by his father. He had always believed his father had been the one to find it, but that was never confirmed. Not too long after the coin was sold, John's father died on a deep dive. The cause was related to the bends.

John continued in his father's footsteps. His education, dives, and recovery efforts were sponsored by the rich entrepreneur who bought the coin. Now, another had come on the scene; another of a coin that was not supposed to exist.

John advised Bill to protect the coin, not to show it to anyone. He would help him discover the truth about it and he knew someone who could help.

Bill held a feeling inside himself that John was an honorable man, someone who could be trusted. He told him he was a retired detective, about Tom Dearing, what he had found out about him, and about the burglary at his home.

"They're after the coin," John said. "They know it has great value, but they don't care about its historic value."

"Its historic value? I don't follow," Bill stated.

"I'll need to contact my friend, maybe set up a meeting so we can figure out where to go from here."

"Now this is starting to sound more cloak and dagger than just a coin inquiry."

"Believe me, in treasure hunting, there are a lot more daggers than cloaks. There are many dangers and not all of them below water."

"I'm starting to believe that," Bill said. "You should have seen my house."

"It may have been a good thing you weren't there. These people can be ruthless."

"Well, so can I," Bill said, "especially when it comes to my family," he said, patting the concealed gun on his side.

"How about I call you tonight or tomorrow after I contact my friend. I'm sure he'll want a meeting real soon. He has a lot of information that I believe you will be interested in."

They exchanged numbers, shook hands once more, and Bill and Sam left the show.

When they got to the car, Bill reminded Sam that he was to tell his mother about all the great things he saw, but nothing about the coin, or John.

"You think we can trust him, Grandpa?" Sam asked.

"Yes, I think we can," Bill returned.

"Me too," Sam said, smiling. "I like him."

"Let's just hope his friend is the same," Bill added.

*

Vickie was enjoying her evening off, knowing she didn't have to get up early. Tomorrow there were no appointments, no pressing leads to run down, no one to lie to her, and hopefully, no one to give her any grief.

She had settled in; slipped into her favorite pajamas, her sore feet in some comfy house shoes, and turned the TV to a classic 1940's movie playing. The spaghetti she fixed was exceptionally good and the wine even better. One more glass before she went to bed would fit just right.

The move, *The Ghost and Mrs. Muir,* which was in black and white, was a great classic, but she had seen it before and it was just on for some background noise while she thumbed through a new magazine. Suddenly, the light she was reading with went out. This one was different from the other light she had problems with on the table at the other end of the couch.

"Great," she complained, "do I have to go around and tighten every bulb?" She sat up, put the magazine down, and scooted over to the end of the couch. She reached up under the lampshade to tighten the bulb and pulled her hand back quickly.

"What the—" she exclaimed, quickly reeling back, staring at the lamp. After a few seconds, she moved over to a position where she could look up under the lampshade. There was no bulb in the lamp.

Vickie was a little rattled, but she was a practical and logical individual. After thinking a bit, she remembered removing the bulb last week after it had burnt out, but she didn't have one to replace it. It slipped her mind while at the store.

She must have been using light from a reflection or some other source to read by and didn't give it much thought. She had been getting drowsy and the wine, not to mention the ghost story, may have played a part in her perception that it had been something unnatural. All logical.

She decided it was time for bed anyway. She shut everything down, brushed her teeth, and crawled into her bed.

Her bed.

Once, it had been their bed.

She said goodnight to her husband and her daughter just as she did every night. She missed them; wanted them. She cried softly as she did most nights, burying her face in the pillow, remembering, until she fell asleep.

And like most nights, she dreamed.

They were all laughing; sitting at a traffic light while on

the way home from dinner at their favorite restaurant. It was their custom when they were all together to make jokes while stopped at red lights. It was fun, made the wait shorter, and gave everyone a chance to interact; family time in a moving, metal box. There was no escape.

Her husband, David, had told a stupid joke. Her daughter, Kristy, sitting in the backseat of the car was not to be outdone, "That joke is so stupid, a rock has a higher IQ."

Vickie and David looked at each other with as straight a face as they could until they both couldn't hold it anymore and both cracked up.

This had been no ordinary Saturday. David, a lieutenant in the Uniform Division took a rare Saturday off. It was Kristy's twelfth birthday and they had taken her to a movie, bowling, and shopping before going to dinner that evening.

"Okay, I heard the greatest knock-knock joke, *ev-ver*," Vickie said. She loved to tell her daughter puns and jokes.

"Oh, I love those," Kristy said.

"Good," Vickie said, "You start it."

"Knock-knock," Kristy said.

"Who's there?" Vickie asked.

"Huh? Wait—what?" That's my line. Isn't it?" A confused Kristie asked.

After a second, they all began to laugh again.

"That was a good one, Mom," Kristy said, still

snickering. "I'll have to remember that one for school on Monday."

The light changed, and Vickie started to pull off. She hadn't gone but just a few feet when a large truck T-boned them on the passenger side.

Vickie's eyes fluttered. A man's voice was talking to her from far away, but it seemed to be getting louder, clearer. He was saying her name she finally realized. She didn't know the voice and she struggled to open her eyes. There was a lot of light and she tried to turn her head away, but she couldn't.

The voice was telling her to wake-up, to open her eyes. With a mighty effort, Vickie did. She opened her eyes to the face of a stranger.

"Don't try to talk. I'm Doctor Bennet. You're in the hospital. You've been in an automobile accident."

Still groggy and with a raspy voice, she managed to ask, "David? Kristy?"

"We'll talk about that in a minute," the doctor stated as he got closer, shining a light into her eye.

Vickie knocked it away, almost pulling over the stand holding the clear-plastic IV pack with the long tube going to her arm.

"Tell me, now," she demanded, her voice getting stronger. "Are they here? Are they okay?"

"Mrs. Winston, you have a concussion," the doctor

informed her. "You have been in a coma for the past three days. I need you to remain calm."

"Tell me," Vickie pleaded.

There was silence.

"Tell me or I swear I'll get out of this bed and find them myself."

The doctor looked at Vickie and began. "I'm sorry, they both—"

Vickie woke-up. She was in her bed, in her apartment. This was the point in the nightmare she usually awoke. Sometimes, it was at the point of the crash, and sometimes it was at the first volley of the Atlanta Police Honor Guard's rifle salute during the funeral.

Every night, Vickie remembered it all.

William N. Gilmore

CHAPTER 35

"Do you really think Jimmy was the one who killed your brother?" Mike asked.

"From what you've told me," Patrick stated with confidence, "it fits like a glove. He was there; he's left-handed; he's quick to use his knife, and he's an Ormond Boy."

"Well, so am I," Mike reminded him. "Or, I was."

"Did you ever kill anyone?"

"No. Of course, not," Mike insisted, shocked, shaking his head quickly. "I couldn't."

"Do you know of anyone else who bragged of stabbing a Liberty Boy?" Patrick asked. "Or, is left-handed?"

"Just Jimmy," Mike had to admit. "But there were others with him when it happened. Jimmy's not likely to start trouble unless he has someone to back him."

"He's a coward, then. More likely to run away when he's alone if confronted."

"He's almost never alone. He has his boys watching his back all the time. Even when he sleeps," Mike added.

"There's one more thing," Patrick stated. "I look a lot like my brother. In fact, many people thought we were twins. Let's see what he has to say when I walk into the saloon."

"I don't think that's such a good idea. He might recognize you."

"That's what I'm hoping. That will confirm to me he killed Aaron. They'll be no doubt."

"The boat leaves in the morning, Pat. Don't do anything to jeopardize missing this opportunity."

"That's why you're staying right here. If anything happens to me, I want you to get to California, find that gold and build the castle overlooking the ocean. I'll show you where I hid the money. Just in case."

"I'm not going without you," Mike pleaded. "You can't stand up to them by yourself. It's just right stupid."

"They know you, they don't know me. I have the advantage," Patrick insisted. "Besides, if they tip their hand, I'll get out of there in a hurry. We'll be on the boat and far away before they can pull up their knickers in the morning."

"What are you going to do to Jimmy? What happens if they grab you and you can't get back in time?"

"As for Jimmy, we'll see. But I will get back."

"And if you don't?" Mike wanted an answer, again.

"I'll try to find you in California. Don't forget, anything you find is half mine. Don't drink it all up."

"I think I may have a change of name," Mike said. "You just better make it back."

"Yeah, it looks like I better."

CHAPTER 36

The telephone rang in Sean's study. It was a separate line from the regular household number.

"Yes?" Sean asked, a bit of luck he was in the study that early when the call came.

"Hey there, Mr. Murphy, this is John."

"Hello, John," Sean answered happily, "it's been a while, but I have told you many times, call me Sean."

"Yes sir, it's just hard for me."

"How have you been, John? Any interesting dives?"

"Well, sir, the most interesting thing happened over at the coin show yesterday. I would really like to meet with you and tell you in person. It's pretty awesome."

"Awesome?" He snickered. "The words you young people use these days."

John got serious. "It's important."

"Sean never knew John to sound so insistent. "Okay, what about next Tuesday. We can—"

"This can't wait." John reiterated.

"Today's Sunday—"

"This will be fine, say about two o'clock? Your place."

"Looks like you've already made up my mind for me,"

Sean stated." Okay. Two it is, and I'm bringing a new friend who has a story you are going to love."

John called Bill Warner, apologized for the short notice and told him about the meeting he had set up, hoping it would not be an inconvenience.

Bill said he would be there and asked if it would be alright to bring Sam with him. John said it should be fine and gave him the address. He also told him not to forget the coin.

Sean trusted John, but he was also a practical man. He looked around his desktop and found the card he was looking for. He called the number.

"Detective Winston," she answered.

"Detective, this is Sean Murphy."

She was very surprised he would be calling her. "Yes, Mr. Murphy, what can I do for you?"

"Would it be possible for you to come by the house today, say around 2 o'clock? I'd like to talk with you."

She was about to tell him it was her day off, but with this opening, she knew she had better jump at the chance while he was willing. "Sure, Mr. Murphy, I'll be looking forward to it." There went her relaxing day and possibly the chance for her not to be lied to. And in the back of her mind, the chance to see the nice and yet, strange little girl.

A few hours later, John was the first to arrive at the Murphy estate, with Bill Warner and Sam pulling in right behind him at the front gate.

John pulled up to an intercom, pushed a button, and after just a few seconds, the gate opened. They continued up a long driveway to the house and parked in a circular drive. They all exited their vehicles and John went up to Bill, shaking his hand.

"Good timing, Mr. Warner," John said, smiling. "I hope you didn't have any problems finding the place."

"No, not at all," Bill said. "I'm familiar with the area." There were few areas Bill was unfamiliar with in Atlanta.

Sam looked at the large house and grounds in awe. "Is this a hotel?" He asked, innocently.

John laughed. "No, this belongs to a friend of mine. He's rich and he lives here. He also owns some buildings downtown."

"Wow!" Sam exclaimed as he continued to admire the site. "You could play a real football game in the front yard."

"True," John admitted, "but you could play a real baseball game in the back."

"Really?" Sam asked.

"Really," John repeated.

"You're to be on your best behavior," Bill told Sam, "and don't touch anything. I probably couldn't afford it if you broke something."

They walked up to the front door and John rang a doorbell. In just a short while, Mrs. Murphy opened the door.

"John, it's so good to see you." She stepped forward,

giving him a hug. "Please, all of you, come in."

"Mrs. Murphy, this is Bill and his grandson, Sam."

"It's a pleasure to meet you," Bill said, shaking hands with her.

Sam also shook hands. "Hello," he said, a little shyly.

"My husband is finishing up in the study and should be right out. He wanted me to let you have a seat in the dining room, there are some refreshments set up there."

They followed her to a large room with a large table, maybe twenty chairs. On the table was a nice spread of food, including glossy, white plates, silverware (real silver), cloth napkins, and a variety of drinks. This wasn't just a setup of refreshments, this was a full-blown, restaurant-quality meal.

"Please, have a seat wherever you wish, I'll see if my husband will be much longer."

At first, Bill wasn't really sure where to sit, which end of the table, or in the middle. John wasn't much help on that and shrugged his shoulders. They compromised and they all sat near one end.

"Grandpa Bill, can I get something to eat?"

"Well, I guess. That's what it's there for. Just be careful, though. Don't drop or spill anything. And use the napkin."

"He does this all the time," John said. "But he's genuine, not trying to show off or anything, and he wants you to feel comfortable. He never tries to be uppity or superior."

"And just who is this guy?" Bill asked.

"I'm Sean Murphy," said a strong voice coming into the dining room.

Bill rose and turned. There was a man, average in almost every way, except he had a bandage on his forehead. "I'm Bill Warner and this is my grandson, Sam."

"Welcome to my home, Mr. Warner, Sam. Hello, John," he reached over and shook his hand as well. "I'm dying to hear what all this is about."

Just then, Mrs. Murphy entered the dining room followed by Vickie Winston. All the men stood.

"Detective, I'm so glad you could join us," Mr. Murphy stated.

Vickie walked in, looking a little confused. "I'm sorry, am I interrupting something?"

"No. Not at all," he said, taking her hand. "I wanted you to be here. I wasn't really sure what I was expecting today. This is my friend and associate, John Gray.

Vickie nodded towards the young man.

"This is—"

"Hello, Bill," the detective said before Mr. Murphy could make the introduction.

"Hello, Vickie," Bill returned.

"Oh, you know each other?" Mr. Murphy asked.

"Yes," Bill said. "From the police department. We've

known each other for many years."

"Darling, would you tell Caution our guests are here," Mr. Murphy asked.

"She's in her room. I'm sure Molly has alerted her, but I'll see if she's ready to come down."

"Detective, please have a seat," Mr. Murphy stated, "We'll get this show on the road in just a few minutes."

"Mr. Murphy, I'm a little confused," Vickie began. "I thought you had wanted to see me, alone, to discuss your case?"

"That's part of it, my wife and I have been talking and there are some other concerns we wanted to discuss. Then this meeting came up and although I trust my friend John, I didn't know anything about who he was bringing. With all the other unpleasantness we've had, I wanted to make sure things were on the up and up."

Caution came running into the dining room and right into Vickie, giving her a big hug. Molly was right behind, dancing around the two.

"I've missed you," Caution said. "Molly did too."

"I've missed you, too," Vickie said, looking at Mrs. Murphy standing in the doorway. She was actually smiling.

"Okay, you know what I've said about Molly being in the dining room," Mr. Murphy stated. "Why don't you take, Sam here for a tour of the house while we have a meeting.

"Okay, Father. Hi, I'm Caution, and this is Molly," she

said. "Would you like to see our house.

"I'd like that. I'm Sam by the way."

"I kind of figured that," she laughed.

The two kids headed out of the dining room.

Vickie took a seat at the table, across from Bill.

"If there's anything you want, just let me know," Mrs. Murphy stated. She closed the double sliding doors to the dining room when she exited.

"Well, John, now that we have all the introductions out of the way, why don't you tell us what we are doing here."

"You did bring it?" John asked, nervously.

"Of course," Bill answered.

"Please, show him," John smiled and nodded his head in Sean's direction.

Bill reached into his pocket and pulled out the plastic coin holder. He slid it across the table to Mr. Murphy.

Sean, not sure what to expect, reached for the coin holder while looking at John. "What have you got here, Bill, a gold Spanish doubloon from a treasure ship you want us to dive on?"

"You better look closely, Sean," John stated.

Murphy held the coin up and saw the British coat of arms. "Okay, so you have a British Sovereign. It looks like it's in pretty good shape."

"And?" John inquired.

He turned the coin over. His eyes opened wide, staring at the coin in disbelief. Then his mouth opened, closed, and opened once more. "It's—it's an 1840," Murphy stuttered.

"What's an 1840?" Vickie asked.

CHAPTER 37

Patrick was headed out of the cabin.

"I still think I should go with you," Mike stated. "How could I forgive myself if something happens to you?"

"It won't be on you, it will be on me and the dirty scoundrel who gets me," Patrick insisted. "If you come along, I won't get the surprise I'm looking for and he'll put us together as chums. That just won't do. He can't know."

"Maybe you should take a knife or better yet, a gun," Mike suggested.

"I can't go in there like I'm looking for trouble."

"Everyone in there will have some kind of weapon," Mike declared. "A knife, pistol, brass knuckles, a sap, something. I could carry it for you."

"No. I won't go with a weapon."

"What if I—" Mike started with another idea.

"No more. I have to do this myself. I need to do it, for Aaron."

"Okay. I'll be waiting right here."

"And I'll be back before you know it," Patrick promised, trying to give his best, sincere smile, hoping Mike didn't see through it as he went out the door.

Patrick walked off the gangplank and headed to
O'Mally's Saloon. He still wasn't sure what he was going to do
when he confronted Jimmy. He was thinking up plans as he
walked along the directions Mike had given him, hoping to come
up with something before he got there.

Every plan he came up with could possibly end up with
him having a big knife in his gut. The only one he had that would
see him sailing off with Mike to California was for him to turn
around. Now.

It was almost too late for that. Just in front of him was the
large building with the big sign; O'Mally's Saloon. For some
reason, he looked down at his feet. There beside his right foot
was a smooth, black, river rock. He reached down and picked it
up. He looked at it a minute, wiped the dirt off it and put it in his
pocket. He took a deep breath and headed for the doors.

*

Big Mike could barely stand it, but he had promised
Patrick he would stay in the cabin until he got back; if he got
back. Mike questioned the decision to let him go, then he
questioned if he even had any right to stop him. There were too
many things going through his oversized head and he wished he
had known the right thing to do.

Somehow, in all that jumbled mess came a pinhole of
clarity. He would ask for forgiveness later.

Patrick walked into the saloon and over to the bar. There

were quite a few people there, but hardly anyone noticed him; this was good, keep a low profile, blend in, keep your eyes open.

This part of the plan was working pretty good. Then the bartender asked him what he wanted.

"Beer," was all Patrick said.

The bartender put a tankard on the bar in front of Patrick. "That'll be ten-cents," he said, not letting go of the tankard.

Patrick reached into his pocket and pulled out a quarter, placing it on the bar. "You can keep the change. Tell me where I can find Jimmy."

The bartender looked Patrick over real good, then without taking his eyes off him, motioned his head towards the back of the saloon. He let go of the tankard and scooped up the quarter, giving a wicked smile.

Just as Mike had described, sitting at a back table, wearing a bowler hat was Jimmy 'The Blade' Dugan; saloon owner, Ormond Boy, and Aaron's killer.

William N. Gilmore

CHAPTER 38

"Is it real?" Sean Murphy asked.

"I don't know much about coins," Bill Warner admitted, "especially foreign ones and I can only tell you how it was found. I'll let the experts make the determination."

"It looks good to me, Mr., ah, Sean. I know there were coins that were reminted, and some were re-struck, but there were never any 1840's re-made or re-dated for that date."

"I'm sorry, but I'm really confused now," Vickie said. "I don't know anything about coins, so what am I doing here?"

"I'll make it clear to you in just a bit, Detective. For now, let's say I need you for our security. I understand this is your off day. I will compensate your time."

"I'm not a security guard, Mr. Murphy. I'm here to follow up on your burglary and your assault."

"You were assaulted?" John asked, surprised.

"It's nothing. They didn't get anything important," Mr. Murphy stated. "Now, back to this coin. Where did you get it, Mr. Warner?"

"Okay, let's start from the beginning," Bill said. "I'll provide you with the information when you tell us what's so special about this coin and what it's all about. You see, my house was burglarized the other day as well; by someone, I'm sure who was looking for this coin after I showed it to what I later learned was a crooked coin dealer," he said, pointing at the coin Mr. Murphy was still holding. "What is it about this thing, anyway?"

"What I'm holding," Mr. Murphy started, "may be one of the most valuable coins in the world, one that is believed to have never existed, yet it was intended to change world history, our history, and the lives of possibly millions of people."

*

Caution was showing Sam around the huge house. He saw the library, the conservatory, the kitchen, the bathrooms (there were a lot of those, and each was as big as his whole bedroom at his mom's house).

"You could play hide and seek in here and never get found," Sam said.

"Molly and I do that all the time. She's too good though and always wins," Caution said.

Molly, standing next to Caution, looked up at her and seemed to be smiling.

"What's your favorite room?" Sam asked.

"Come on, I'll show you."

He followed her up the stairs to a bedroom. It was ginormous.

"This is my room. It's my favorite of all, but let me show

you my favorite place in the whole world."

Caution went to the far end of her room and opened double doors to the outside. There was a very large balcony she walked out on that overlooked the back of the estate. It was a beautiful sight. She walked out to the far edge of the balcony, and the wind swirled around her, throwing her long, red hair all around.

Molly was dancing at her side, enjoying the wind in her own way, spinning in circles, sniffing for odors, strange and familiar.

"Come on," Caution said, motioning with her hands, "don't be scared, it's delightful."

"I'm not scared of anything," Sam said, looking a little unsure. Still, he slowly made his way to where Caution was standing. "You have a really big backyard. How high are we?"

"It's as high as a kite flies," Caution said, laughing. "Isn't it great? The wind comes rushing through like you're on a roller coaster, but you're standing still.

Sam put his face to the wind, his own hair was being swished back and forth and once, he almost had to catch his balance. "It's nice. I like it."

"This is my favorite place in the world," Caution reiterated. "It makes me feel good when I'm sad, or when I need to think, or just because. Sometimes, when my Grandpa Patrick is here, we look out and pretend we can see across the ocean all the way to Ireland. That was his home before crossing the ocean in a big ship to come here. That was a long time ago."

"I learned about Ireland in school," Sam said, "but I've only seen pictures of it in books. It's really green."

"My Grandpa told me all about it. Maybe I'll see it one day."

Sam looked out trying to imagine the faraway land.

Caution broke that gaze. "At night, when you turn off all the lights, you can see so many stars."

"I know almost all of the constellations," Sam stated, bragging a little. "My Grandpa Bill taught me."

"Me too," Caution said, proudly. "My Grandpa Patrick taught me."

They laughed.

"Aren't grandpa's great?" Sam said as a statement more than a question. "My Grandpa Bill is my mom's father."

"Where's your dad?" Caution asked.

"He left when I was really young," Sam said. "He wasn't very nice to my mom. I don't remember him much."

"I'm sorry," Caution said.

"I've got Grandpa Bill, though. He's the greatest. I get to go stay with him a lot. Where's your grandpa?"

"He comes around as much as he can," Caution said, careful not to give away any secrets Grandpa Patrick told her to keep. "Let's go, I'll show you outside."

CHAPTER 39

Sean Murphy had excused himself from the table and returned just a few minutes later. He was carrying a wooden box and a couple long circular cases. He put these on the table and opened the box, removing something.

"Mr. Warner, may I call you Bill, this is the only other sample of an 1840 British Sovereign that I know to exist, what I believed was the only one, until today." He handed him a plastic enclosed case with a coin that was the twin of his.

I think yours is in a little better shape," Bill said, examining the coin very closely.

"Not by much," Sean said. "You were going to tell us how you came to find yours."

"I didn't find it, my grandson, Sam did."

"Sam?" Sean asked, surprised.

"We were on vacation and he was using a metal detector on the beach. He said it was only a few inches down, which surprised me."

"That last big storm we had on the coast must have churned some things up," John said. "It happens all the time. Spanish silver, sometimes jewel-encrusted rings and necklaces, even parts of ships wash up if the storm is big enough."

"I have some old maps here. Bill, can you show us the location where Sam found the coin?"

Bill hesitated for a few seconds. "I'm not sure I'm ready to give that information away. Not until I know more concerning what you said about changing history and such. I believe I'm holding an ace while the cards are still being dealt. I'm still not sure what all this is about."

"All right, Bill, I understand, and I would be skeptical if I were in your shoes too, so in full disclosure, and to give you and the detective here some background, let me tell you a story, a story that started over a hundred and seventy-five years ago."

Sean proceeded to give Bill and Vickie a quick history lesson on the anti-slavery movement, both here, in this young country and in the British Empire, decades before the American Civil War, without getting into the politics and causes of the war.

He told them about the secret support England was going to give, sending a stockpile of gold from its treasury on an unregistered ship and how Joseph Long and the ship disappeared.

"If all this was secret and Joseph Long supposedly went down with the ship, how do you know about it?" Bill asked.

"And how do you know Joseph Long or someone else didn't steal the gold at some point? Vickie asked.

"Because there was a survivor, only one, who knew about the gold, Joseph Long, and where the ship sank."

"Why haven't I heard about this before?" John asked.

"Because it's something I wanted to keep secret until the time was right. You see, he was washed up on shore, badly injured, and lasting only a few days. As a delirious man, he rambled, talking strangely, telling only one person what he knew before he died. The story was suspect and the delusions of a man about to meet his maker. At first, they were discarded."

"Who did he tell?" John asked.

"My great-grandmother, Esther Murphy, when she was a young girl, nursing him. She only confided the information to her husband, Patrick years later. He put it into a journal."

"That is some story," Bill said. "So, you believe there is a treasure of gold out there somewhere on the ocean bottom and all you have is a coin, maybe two, that came from that shipwreck, and the third-hand account of the ramblings of a dying man.?"

"No. I didn't say that was all I had. You see, that ship went down in 1840 in an area I've been trying to map. Strange as it might seem, my great-grandfather, Patrick Murphy, was on another ship that sunk in the exact same location in 1850. Many years later, Patrick Murphy hired a man to look for some of the chests from the 1850's wreck. That was John's great-grandfather."

"My great-grandfather?" John asked. "So, that's how my family got started in the business."

"The diving technology at the time was crude; diving helmets, hand pumps for air, the bends were common if the water was too deep. He didn't find the chests, but he did find a single coin. An 1840 British Sovereign. This one, to be exact," Sean said, holding up his coin. "He kept it and passed it on to his grandson, whom I bought it from."

"It was my great-grandfather who found the coin? They never told me. Why not?"

"Over the many years," Sean continued, "there had been much speculation and many rumors about the 1840 Sovereigns, the shipwreck, and possible treasure. There were some bad people trying to get information on it, some who would do some pretty nasty things. I think they were trying to protect you."

"Is this why your house was burglarized, and you were assaulted?" Vickie asked.

"I think so. There's not any other reason besides the treasure. They were after the coin for sure, possibly the journal. I don't know how much information they have."

"What would that be worth in today's money?" Vickie asked.

"From 1840, one million dollars adjusting for inflation for today, I'd say between $25,000,000 to $30,000,000. But that's not the gold or historic value. I'd say it's closer to half a billion."

"That's a lot of motive," Vickie stated.

"That's another reason you are here, Detective. I want you to keep my family safe."

"That's not—I work for the Atlanta Police Department, I can't provide personal service to one family. Bedside's I'm a Burglary Detective. What you need is a professional personal protection outfit."

"I've done my homework, Detective Winston, I know your background. I know you were on the mayor's protection unit during her eight years in office. You have enough time on the force to retire if you wanted. I know you lost your husband and daughter to a drunk driver, you live alone, and have no other romantic or family relationships."

"How dare you," Vickie uttered." My personal life is my own. You have no right."

"Forgive me, Detective," Mr. Murphy stated humbly, "I'm a rich man and I usually get what I want, but I am also a businessman, a careful man, especially when it comes to my family, so, before I offer you the job, I do my checking."

"Job?" Vickie questioned. "What job?"

"I want you to come work for me to protect my wife and my daughter. I'll set up your own private account, hire whomever you feel you can trust, get the equipment you need. I'll double your salary plus benefits."

Vickie looked at Mr. Murphy in disbelief. Her mouth was open, but nothing came out.

"You don't have to answer right now, but I'll need it soon."

"Okay," Vickie answered softly, flabbergasted.

"Bill, are you interested in selling me your coin?"

"Well—" Bill was unsure how to answer.

"Think about it, come up with a number, and we'll do business. Also, I'll include you in the partnership."

"What partnership?" Bill asked.

"All of you," he said pointing at everyone. "All of us," he said, moving his finger around in a circle.

"What kind of partnership are you talking about, Mr. Murphy?" Vickie asked. "I don't have any money to invest if that's what you are talking about."

"You won't need to, I'm taking care of everything."

"Taking care of what?" Bill asked.

"We're going after the rest of the shipwrecked treasure, of course."

"Which shipwreck, "John asked, "the 1840 or the 1850?"

"Both," Sean laughed. "Now, please, eat. There is so much more to talk about."

No one moved. They were all looking at each other in disbelief.

"What just happened?" Vickie broke the silence.

"Congratulations. I think you have a new job," Bill said, "and we all have become pirates, partner."

CHAPTER 40

Patrick walked over to the table Jimmy was sitting behind. He didn't say anything, just looked at him.

Jimmy looked at the young man, cocked his head and seem to have a gleam of recognition in his eye.

"Do I know ye from somewheres?" Jimmy asked, cocking his head the other way.

"When you stab somebody in the gut, maybe you should check to see if you did a right fine job of it," Patrick stated.

Jimmy's eyes got big as saucers. He started to reach for his knife and Patrick kicked the table, pinning Jimmy to the wall with his arms unable to move. The back of his head hit the wall so hard, his bowler sprang up like the top of his head popped.

Patrick kept his foot pressed on the table, keeping the pressure of the table on Jimmy's chest with him unable to go for his knife.

One of Jimmy's Boys ran to rescue him, but Patrick picked up a large tankard from the table and smashed him in the face, causing him to drop right there.

Patrick took his foot down and now pushed with both hands on the table. No one else approached him.

"Out," Patrick commanded. "Everyone out, and take him

with you," he said of the unconscious lad.

There was a scramble for the door, some moving a little quicker than others. Within thirty seconds, everyone was out.

"Ye should have died," Jimmy said. "If not the cut, the bloody infection should have did ye in."

"It did. I suffered every day and died a week later," Patrick said, keeping up the charade.

All color left Jimmy's face. "Mother Mary, Mother of God," Jimmy prayed loudly, slamming his eyes shut.

"That won't do you no bloody good. Your fate is sealed, you maggot. I've been sent to collect your foul, black soul."

"Saint Christopher, protect me," Jimmy cried out, still not opening his eyes.

Patrick pulled the table away from Jimmy, but Jimmy didn't move. Patrick got up to the side of his head and whispered in his ear. Jimmy opened his eyes and looked at something Patrick was showing him. Jimmy threw his arms up across his face and let out a sorrowful moan.

Patrick reached in and removed Jimmy's big knife from his belt without any resistance.

"Stand up," Patrick demanded.

Jimmy didn't move except for his sobbing.

Patrick grabbed him by his collar, lifting him to his feet. The bowler dropped to the floor as Jimmy crossed himself several times then covered his face with his hands, stifling the sobs coming from the broken person who had once been Jimmy Dugan.

Patrick took the knife and cut the suspender straps holding up Jimmy's pants. He cut his shirt right up the back and had him strip it off.

Patrick dragged Jimmy to the front door of the saloon and kicked him out into the street. Everyone who had been inside the saloon and a small crowd of onlookers had gathered there and watched as Jimmy got to his feet and ran off screaming, his knickers gathered around his ankles causing him to trip several times.

That was the last time anyone saw Jimmy Dugan alive.

William N. Gilmore

CHAPTER 41

Caution and Sam came back inside the large house and went to the dining room to see if the meeting was still going on. Grandpa Bill was at one end of the table with Caution's father, looking over a map.

Grandpa Bill noticed the two kids and called Sam over. "Mr. Murphy has a coin like the one you found, Sam. Is it alright if I tell him where you found it?"

"He does?" Sam asked, a hopeful grin on his face. "Is it real pirate treasure?"

"It sure is, Sam." Mr. Murphy stated.

"Wow!" Sam said, a big smile on his face. "I knew it."

"Well?" Grandpa Bill asked. "It's up to you. What do you say?"

"Do I have to give up my coin, Grandpa?" Sam asked, a little disappointment in his voice.

"Not if you don't want to," Grandpa Bill said, looking over at Sean, shrugging his shoulders.

"Sam, that coin is yours," Mr. Murphy stated. "You found it. No one can take that away from you. Just promise me something."

"Yes, sir?"

"If you ever decide to sell it, for whatever reason, please let me be the first to make you an offer. Keep it safe, don't show it or tell anyone about it. It's not just a coin, it's history."

"Okay," Sam agreed.

"Now, would you like to help us find some more coins?" Mr. Murphy asked.

"You're going to find *more*?" Sam asked, an even bigger smile crossing his face as he looked over at Grandpa Bill, who was nodding his head.

"That's the plan," Mr. Murphy said, "and you my young, pirate treasure-finding friend, are part of that plan."

"And Grandpa Bill?" Sam asked.

"Grandpa Bill, Vickie, John, Mrs. Murphy and myself, and Caution too," he said with a laugh.

"And don't forget Molly," Caution reminded him.

"Yes, Molly too," Mr. Murphy agreed.

Molly gave a quick bark that seemed to seal the deal.

They all laughed.

After the meeting, Vickie and Bill walked together to their cars while Sam was saying goodbye to Caution and Molly at the front door.

"Well, what are you going to do?" Bill asked.

"I don't have a clue," Vickie said. "It's all so sudden. What do you think I should do?"

"That's not my decision," Bill shook his head. "Why

don't you go home and think about it. Weigh your options."

"Twice my salary on top of my pension," Vickie mused, "plus benefits, that's an offer hard to refuse."

"And you'll have your own account to get the people and equipment you'd need. Sounds sweet," Bill said.

"Why don't you take it, Bill? Right up your alley."

"He didn't offer it to me, besides, and no offense, but I have a family to think about, to take care of. I can't just go or respond at a moment's notice and can you see me trying to tell two women what to do? I want to keep my sanity intact."

"He did say I could hire those I trusted. Want a job?"

"Does that mean you're taking it?"

"I'll let you know in a couple days. My head is about to explode."

"What do you think of this 'partnership' he wants everyone to belong to?" Bill asked.

"Treasure," she laughed. "It most likely would be a wild goose chase anyway," Vickie replied. "Maybe, even dangerous."

"Half a billion dangerous," Bill agreed. "Sam, it's time to go," he called out."

"Why don't you come over tomorrow night, I'll fix dinner, we can talk about it."

"Why, Detective Winston, are you asking me on a date?"

"Ahh—no, nothing like that," she said, now embarrassed and turning red. "Like a partnership meeting, that's all," she threw in, recovering most of her composure.

"What time?" Bill asked.

A few minutes later, Vickie drove off and Sam came running up to Grandpa Bill, grabbing him around the waist.

"Are we really going to find the pirate treasure," he asked, overly excited.

"It sure looks that way. I'm not sure yet what our part will be. We won't be doing any of the diving I'm afraid and we may not even get back to that same area where you found your coin. It looks like John will be handling most of the search operation under Mr. Murphy's direction."

"Aww, I wanted to help go look for it," Sam said, disappointed. "Use my metal detector again."

"Somehow, I knew that but look, you have a new-found friend and maybe we can come visit again real soon."

"I'd like that. She's nice and so are her mom and dad. Maybe we'll meet her grandpa, too. Caution says he doesn't come over as much as he used to."

"Her grandfather?" Grandpa Bill inquired.

"Her Grandpa Patrick," Sam said as he got in the car.

They never noticed the dark SUV just down the street, nor the men inside. One was watching them through binoculars while the other took photos with a camera equipped with a long telephoto lens.

CHAPTER 42

Patrick left the saloon without being harassed or anyone following him. He didn't think it would have been in their best interest anyway.

"Drinks are on the house," he called over his shoulder. The street was clear in just a few seconds.

He made his way back to the boat and to the cabin where Mike was sitting on his bunk, wiping a dirty face, sweat beading on his brow, and breathing heavily.

"Well?" Mike asked, still trying to catch his breath.

"I didn't hardly touch him," Patrick gave a true account. "And what's with you, all huffin' and puffin' like you got the bloody croup. Did you go somewhere, Mike?"

"Who, me?" Mike tried to play innocent.

"No, that bloody mouse over in the corner."

Mike quickly turned, but there was no mouse. "You're just trying to josh me," he said with a worried smile.

"Mike, what did you do? Tell me right now."

"I couldn't just sit here," Mike said.

"That's exactly what I told you to do."

"But that's not right. We're partners now. I had to go, I'm sorry. I had to make sure you didn't get into any trouble."

"I didn't see you," Patrick stated, confused.

"I, ah—I disguised myself. "I put some mud on my face, a scarf over my head, and wrapped a blanket around me like those injun's do. I didn't talk to nobody, I just grunted. I ran to the saloon and everybody was coming out. I snuck over to the side window and watched."

"What did you see?" Patrick asked.

"Jimmy had his arms over his face and the table pushed into his gut. You pulled the table back and took Jimmy's knife out of his belt. He didn't even flinch. I thought you were going to slice him up good, but instead, you made him look at something and said something in his ear. I saw you toss him out on the street nearly naked and he ran off like a scalded dog. I ran back here to the boat to get here before you did. I just made it.

"So, you can see I didn't need you to worry about me. You don't have to be my protector all the time, Mike."

"Okay, I get it," Mike stated. "But there's something I just have to know; what did you show him and what did you say in his ear, Patrick, that had him so bloody scared?"

"Let's put that part behind us for now," Patrick stated. "I want to forget all about this mess. Rest, and eat something."

"Me too," Mike agreed. "I'm hungry, now. But sometime, I want to hear the whole story."

"You're hungry? Imagine that," Patrick laughed, now changing the subject. "You had better eat up good, tomorrow, we start afresh, the beginning of a new adventure."

"Yeah, but it's not starting out on land. I hate it," Mike declared.

"Well, at least you're starting it with your head above water. You'll never be out of sight of land."

"Lord, let's keep it that way," Mike prayed, crossing himself "And let's not run into any more of the Ormond Boys."

"Amen on that," Patrick said, nodding.

William N. Gilmore

CHAPTER 43

Vickie tossed in her bed and couldn't sleep. It had nothing to do with bad dreams. She was thinking of her future; the police department, retirement, Mr. Murphy's offer, treasure, and somewhere in all of that, Bill Warner.

Was it a date? Was that what she intended? She hadn't been out with anyone since—it had been a long time. Was she ready? Was it cheating on their memory?

She liked Bill. She had known him for almost twenty years. She had even met his wife and daughter while attending several police functions. Each had attended the funeral of the other's family members when tragedy struck only months apart, offering to help in any way.

Maybe it was time. They had a lot in common. She could do much worse than Bill.

Okay, she had to get him off her mind. She had some serious things to consider. Did she want to retire? Well, it wouldn't really be retirement if she was still working, especially if she was being paid twice her salary. Plus, benefits, along with the police pension. Wow.

But it shouldn't be just about money. Doing a protection gig on a mother-daughter would be demanding at best and from the looks of things, possibly dangerous. There was no telling how long the job would last and what if, just perchance, there was a treasure; what then?

She was glad Bill was coming over, so she could get some advice. He always seemed so cool under pressure, level-headed, and cute.

"Wait—what, did I just think 'cute'?" she questioned herself. "Okay, Winston, get him off your mind like that."

It took a long time before she finally fell asleep and dreamed, but for the first time in forever, it wasn't one that would wake her up in the middle of the night.

*

Bill Warner couldn't sleep either. He laid there looking at the ceiling, an open book on his chest. He now held the means to take care of his daughter and grandson with a single coin, if he sold it, or rather, if Sam sold it. And to think, there could be many more, or then again, maybe not.

He was in a strange partnership with a group of people he hardly knew, except for Vickie. Vickie had a hard decision to make. Should she retire from the department now, with a chance to become a wealthy woman, if the treasure exists and if it is found? Just the offer of twice her salary would be very tempting, but how long would the job last?

He knew what she was wanting and hoped he would be able to give her some good advice when they had their date.

Dinner. He meant dinner. Just dinner. It's not going to be a date; just a meeting—with dinner. That's all. But—maybe?

He had to admit, there was an attraction there and it had been there for years, but for some reason, he never acted on it. Maybe he still felt loyalty to his wife, although many years had passed. Maybe he had become comfortable with himself and his family only and wasn't interested in another relationship.

None of this made sense, because he was looking forward to seeing Vickie. He was a little nervous, but excited and willing to see where it might go.

*

Sam was in his bed at his house, fast asleep, dreaming of pirates and chest's full of treasure. It wasn't the first time, but this time it was based on something real, something even the grown-ups believed in.

*

Caution wasn't in bed yet, she was standing out on her balcony staring up at the constellations, the wind was just barely moving, the slow breeze softly caressing her cheek, or perhaps, it was Grandpa Patrick kissing her goodnight.

William N. Gilmore

CHAPTER 44

The boys awoke at first light, got dressed, and headed out to watch the sendoff. The boat would be underway any time now. One of the crew came up to them.

"The captain would like to talk to you," he told Patrick," he looked over at Mike, "both of you. He's up there," he said pointing to the wheelhouse.

"Okay, "Patrick replied. "What's it about?"

"I'm not in the know," he said." none of my business."

Patrick and Mike went up to the wheelhouse, where the boat was steered. It was a large area with a wheel taller than Mike. It was a room of windows and you could see all around.

The boys waited at the door until the captain noticed them and waved them in.

"The constable sent a note to hold the boat for a while until a matter could be straightened out. Seems there was a situation over at O'Mally's Saloon yesterday.

"It was me," Patrick stated. "I confronted the man who was running the saloon. He killed my brother in Dublin," Patrick admitted.

"Did you kill him?" The captain asked. "Was it revenge or self-defense?"

"Neither," Patrick swore. "I didn't hardly touch him. He ran off."

"That's true," Mike confirmed. "I saw it myself."

"So, it was both of you there. You both are involved."

"No. Mike didn't do anything. In fact, I didn't even know he was there."

"And just how did you know your brother's killer was in that particular saloon?" The captain asked, eyeing Patrick.

"Mike told me. He had been there earlier and saw him."

"How did you happen to know this bloke he killed," the captain asked.

"He was part of a gang in Dublin, the Ormond Boys."

"And I didn't kill him," Patrick stated, once again. "What happened to him?"

"He was hung, maybe by his own hand. They say his eyes were gouged out," The captain gave the gory description.

"Not by me," Patrick said strongly.

"Nor me," Mike added.

"So, you went after an Ormond Boy," the captain continued. "What gang did you belong to?"

"I didn't belong to a gang. My brother was part of the Liberty Boys and got stabbed by Jimmy," Patrick told him.

"Jimmy? Jimmy 'The Blade', is that who you're talking about?"

"Isn't that who you're talking about?" Patrick asked.

"You killed Jimmy 'The Blade', all by yourself?"

"I keep telling you, I didn't kill him," Patrick almost yelled.

"Well, the constable may differ with you, and we ain't got time to argue with him." He went to the door and yelled at one of the crew. "Get ready the ropes." The crewman ran off barking orders and several men suddenly attended the moorings.

The captain went to a tube and called down. "Get the boilers back up to full."

"Captain, what's going on?" Patrick asked.

"We're getting underway. No need to wait any longer, we're behind now. Luckily, the boilers had been fired earlier just before we were ordered to wait. It will only take a few minutes to get full steam and we can push off."

"What about the constable?" Mike asked.

"Sounds to me like your friend here is completely innocent and probably did the world a favor."

"Why would you do this, captain? You could get into a lot of trouble," Patrick asked.

"Once a Liberty Boy, always a Liberty Boy," the captain said, smiling and giving a tip of his cap.

William N. Gilmore

CHAPTER 45

Bill Warner took a deep breath, ran his fingers through his hair trying to make sure it didn't look unkempt, said a quick, little prayer, and knocked on the apartment door. To him it seemed like forever before the door opened.

"Hi, Bill, thanks for coming," Vickie said. "Please, come in."

She was wearing a beautiful red dress, a front 'V' cut, fashionably low enough without being gaudy or too revealing. Her hair draped her shoulders while her earrings dangled, sparkling in the light.

Bill was dressed in dark slacks with a medium blue shirt and wearing a solid dark red tie that almost matched her dress.

Neither was dressed for a partnership meeting.

"Since this is dinner, I brought a little something for us to try." He held up a nice bottle of wine, not the convenience store or the pick-up by the cash register type.

"That's so thoughtful of you, thanks. I hope you're hungry," she said, taking the bottle into the kitchen.

"I sure am," he said, then thought that sounded suggestive and was glad she couldn't see his face turning red.

"Have a seat, I'll be with you in a minute. Just a few last

minute things and dinner will be ready in about ten minutes or so." *Oh, God*, she was so nervous. *I said 'minute' three times in two seconds,* she said to herself.

"No problem," Bill said, taking a seat on the couch in the living room. "May I help with anything?"

"No, everything's about ready. How's your grandson taking everything?" she asked from the kitchen, trying to get over being edgy. "Have you talked any with him about what's going on?"

"A little. He seems to be okay with us doing this," Bill returned. "It's all a little new to me, too. It's been a long while. I haven't told my daughter, yet though."

"I still don't know what to tell Mr. Murphy," Vickie said.

"Murphy?" Bill sounded confused, then it hit him. "Oh, yes, him. Of course."

"Vickie stuck her head out of the kitchen, "That is what you were talking about, right?"

"Ehh, yes, yes." *Oh, what an idiot I am.* Bill tried to regain his composure. "Sam's excited, but I told him it's still in the early stages."

Bill looked over at the table at the end of the couch. There was a picture of Vickie's husband and daughter. *What the heck are you doing here, Bill?* He started to excuse himself and apologize for encroaching upon the remembrance of her family.

She walked into the living room and held her hand out to

him. "Dinner is ready," she said with a smile. "I'm so glad you are here. Thank you." She guided him to the table.

"Besides my daughter, I haven't had anyone cook for me in a long time. Thank You.

Bill pulled the chair out for Vickie as she sat and then took the seat next to her.

She took his hand and smiled, which surprised him for a second. She bowed her head and began to say Grace.

He wasn't about to go anywhere real soon.

*

Sean Warner and John Gray were bent over some old maps, making a few calculations.

"Why did you want to begin a partnership with people you hardly know, with no investment from them?" John asked.

"I don't do things on impulse, John. I know what I'm doing," Sean said. "Each and every one of them has something to offer or can do something I need to make this adventure a success. You are unique in what you can do, John. You are irreplaceable."

"But to make them a partner in a salvage operation, which is big bucks if you hit, but if you miss, you're taking on a lot of responsibility and expense for them and I'm not sure I understand."

"It's not just a salvage operation as you call it. This could be world changing."

"I'm not sure, even if we find what you are looking for, it would be cost-effective," John stated

"Let me worry about the bottom line. Remember when you were going to school and even while you were on summer breaks, you would research those old wrecks? That was hit and miss. But you found one that paid for several summers to come. Then you found another. I invested in you, John, not the wrecks. To me, you have never been hit or miss. You've been a hit all the time. I saw that in you when I dealt with your father and you were by his side. I see that in this group. Yes, they are an unknown entity; inexperienced, and uninterested in the research like I was in the beginning, but I still believe in them, in us."

"I trust your instincts, Sean, but there is more going on than just this group working together, going on an adventure, and looking through old books and maps. This is real and there have been some things going on that could put any one of them or all of us in real danger. You still show the scars of that. I just want everyone to know what they are getting into. And one more thing; I want to know everything you do about this operation. I don't want to be left in the dark anymore, it's not fair to me."

"You're right, John, I haven't been totally open with you. I believed it was too dangerous to put all the information out, and it looks like I was right at the time, but now, you can't operate or stay safe without full knowledge. Let's grab some coffee, get comfortable, and I'll tell you everything I know," he said, patting the journal.

*

Tom Dearing was waiting on a report from his man in the field. He had him keeping eyes on Bill Warner and the kid, following them over the past couple days.

When he finally got the call, his man gave him what he had observed so far.

"When they went into the hotel conference center, I saw them talk with several people, but it appeared the shipwreck guy was the one they were most interested in. I couldn't get close enough though to hear what they were saying."

"How about later?" Dearing asked.

"When Warner and the kid went to the estate house, I saw the shipwreck guy again. Then I saw that pretty detective drive in the gate a little later. They all stayed a pretty long time. When they started to leave, I followed Warner and the kid to a house. Must have been the kid's house, because Warner left a short time later without him. Warner drove back to his house and didn't go anywhere until tonight. Guess where he showed up? At the detective dame's apartment, all dressed up and with a bottle. He's still there.

Dearing gave orders to maintain the surveillance and to contact him if anything warranted it or if he had been discovered.

William N. Gilmore

CHAPTER 46

They were on the Ohio moving along with the current and at a great speed. The lookouts, keeping their eyes open for snags and sandbars would yell out if something was spotted in the water.

The boat was fully loaded with bales of cotton and other cargo on the deck and its hold was stuffed with everything from a pre-fab house to bottles of pickles to clothing and shoes to muskets and tools. Things people down-river had ordered and needed to keep their little establishments going or items merchants stocked their shelves with.

If the riverboats stopped, the communities they serviced would die, literally.

Patrick and Mike were lucky to have their own stateroom. Many of the over two-hundred passengers stayed on the cargo deck or in steerage, which was not meant for comfort. Horses, mules, cattle and other animals shared the deck as well.

Many boats that traveled the rivers were large, some were three-hundred to four-hundred feet long and could hold over four-hundred passengers and cargo. They had elaborate dining rooms, smoking rooms, barrooms and even areas for gambling.

The boats, many of which had been built at Pittsburgh,

cost sometimes as much as hundreds of thousands of dollars and were an investment not just for the owners, but the pilots and crew. Investors bought shares in the boats they thought would bring in the biggest profit.

Sometimes, boats could be paid off in a single season of hauling goods and passengers, but sometimes, the boat might catch a snag, catch fire, or a boiler could explode ending the boat's mission or worse, sending it to the bottom of the river.

Boiler explosions caused many a ship to sink and killed hundreds of people, sometimes all at once. When the boats were docked, errant fires could catch cotton or other cargo on fire sending embers traveling from boat to boat, maybe taking dozens at one time.

There were many superstitions among the steamboaters. A white horse was thought to be bad luck, but a white horse brought on board by a preacher was even worse. Black cats and even rats were okay, but a white cat meant bad news. Colors, names, and even numbers caused fears. You would be hard-pressed to find a stateroom numbered 'thirteen' or a boat with a name containing thirteen letters.

As the boats traveled down the rivers, it was common to see Indian camps along the banks and occasionally, someone would be waving a white cloth up and down to get picked up for passage up river. If they waved it side to side, they wanted to go down river.

Most boats didn't travel at night because of the snags and sandbars hidden by the dark. They would tie-up for the night on the banks or had a pre-arranged location where they could take on supplies like food, water, and coal for the furnaces. If they had to travel at night, which was not often, long poles with lanterns attached were hung off the bow of the boat.

As much strain and stress the boats were placed under, it wasn't hard to believe that most didn't last more than five years in service. However, without the steamboat era, this country would not have expanded as quickly as it did, if it would have done so at all.

The steamboat had several advantages over the railroad; they had a natural route that didn't have to be built, the cost was cheaper, and it took less time to get to your destination if it happened to be on or near another waterway, as most large towns had been established.

William N. Gilmore

CHAPTER 47

The dinner went smoothly with talk about everything from Sam to Dearing; including treasure, Sean Murphy, his wife, and their daughter, Caution.

Bill opened the bottle of wine after having just a little trouble with the corkscrew. Vickie guided him, giving directions like a pro. She was. A collection of corks in a kitchen drawer proved it.

He poured a bit in her glass to taste. She sipped it and gave a nod of approval. After filling both glasses, he followed her into the living room where they sat on the couch. He was glad he was sitting at the end with his back to the picture of her husband and child.

"What do you think I should do, Bill?" Vickie asked. She wasn't at the other end of the couch, she had sat not even a foot away from him, now facing him.

"I can't make that decision for you, Vickie," he said. He could smell the sweet fragrance of her perfume and wanted to inhale deeply, but dared not, not yet.

"I knew you would say that," she sounded a little disappointed. "I'm just asking for a little advice, not for you to direct my life. Help me figure this out, please."

"Okay. Let's divide this into pros and cons," he began. "Let's start with the pros."

"Sounds good to me," she said, smiling.

"First, you get to retire."

"Well, that's a given," she said, "but it won't be a real retirement."

"No. But you get to start drawing your full pension, which probably is better than mine. Second, you start right away with your new job at twice your police salary. Pretty nice."

"Well, Mr. Murphy and I haven't gotten into the real particulars of that yet."

"Maybe not, but it seems he's willing to do what he has to do to get you into that job," Bill stated, "benefits and all."

Vickie moved just a little closer to Bill. He had his hand on his knee and she reached over and put her hand on top of his.

"You know, it would make my decision so much easier if you'd agree to come with me on this."

He swallowed hard before speaking, but he didn't move his hand.

"I've been thinking on this a little. There's still a lot we don't know about this so-called partnership Mr. Murphy volunteered us into. We need to sit down with him and get some straight answers. Sam will be totally disappointed if I don't follow through on this. However, he'll be back in school soon and he may forget all about it."

"Oh, I doubt that," Vickie said with a laugh.

"Yeah, I know," Bill acknowledged. "I don't want to put him in any danger, either. All this stuff going on; the secrecy, the burglaries, the assault on Mr. Murphy, and why does he want to hire you to protect his wife and daughter? Is there something he's not telling us?"

"You're right, of course. We need to know everything before we jump into it. Make sure everything is on the up and up, he's a businessman, maybe we need to have contracts."

"That's good thinking," Bill said, "get everything documented, on paper so there is no misunderstanding."

"And there is one more thing," Vickie said, her hand still on his. "I don't want you to work for me."

"Oh, you've changed your mind?" Bill cocked his head, a little confused.

"I want you to work with me," she said, looking into his eyes. "I want us to be equals."

"We haven't even gotten into the cons yet," Bill said. "Even if this job gets up and running, you don't know how long it might last. It could only be a couple weeks or stretch into a few months. Would that be worth your retiring now?"

"Another reason for a contract. Get a guaranteed number of weeks for pay, even if the job expires, if we get fired, or injured, all that stuff and more."

"What if they do find a treasure, do we automatically get

a share or a percentage?" Bill asked.

"That would be nice," Vickie stated, smiling and nodding her head. "See, there are a lot of questions to ask. I'm not going to commit to anything until I get those answers. I still have some cases to work at the department anyway."

"I guess we both have things to think about," Bill said, "I'll call Mr. Murphy and set up another meeting as soon as we can."

Vickie just realized she still had her hand on Bill's and quickly removed it. "More wine?" She asked.

"No, I better not, I'm driving," Bill reminded her.

"But you have such good connections with the police," Vickie said.

"Yes, I do at that," Bill said as he handed her his glass. They both laughed.

The conversation between Bill and Vickie turned towards people on the department, cases they had worked, and other mundane things, staying away for the most part from the large elephant in the room, each other.

"It's starting to get a little late," Bill said, getting up. "You still have a job to go to in the morning so, I think it's time for me to get myself home."

"Don't remind me," Vickie said, standing. "Maybe I should retire, right in the middle of a big case. Would serve them right."

"Is that you, or is that the wine talking?"

"If it's the wine talking, I think it would ask you to stay." She suddenly realized what she said and put her hand over her mouth.

Bill laughed. "Another glass and I probably would, maybe even without another glass, but only if it were you asking."

"I'm sorry, Bill," Vickie said, barely moving her hand from her mouth, her eyes wide, "that came out wrong."

"Did it now?" Bill returned, feeding on the faux pas. "Maybe we'll explore that a little more closely next time."

"Next time?" Vickie sounded almost disappointed and excited at the same time.

"Oh, yes, this was really nice, and I had a great time, however, you've got work tomorrow and I have things to do, so I'm sure there's going to be a next time, partner." Bill gently took her by the shoulders and kissed Vickie on the cheek leaving her standing in her living room as he headed out the door.

She stood there stunned for a few seconds after the door closed behind him. She touched the cheek where he kissed her, thought for just a few seconds about 'next time' and started for the kitchen with a big smile across her blushed face. Then it hit her, she stopped, turned towards the door Bill just went through and stared. "Partner?" She said, out loud.

William N. Gilmore

CHAPTER 48

The trip down the Ohio was mostly calm, far smoother than the rolling ship at sea. The boys usually stayed to themselves, however, occasionally they would go out on deck to see the sights, for Mike to see land, get some fresh air, or eat at the dining room.

During some of the excursions on deck, Patrick would write in the journal, recalling some of the times he had in Ireland, how he met Mike, the wreck of the ship they sailed on, and the finding of the gold, or things he just wanted to write down.

Sometimes, they would see the remnants of steamboats and other vessels that had sunk, or that had been destroyed by fire along the banks or caught up on a sandbar reminding them how dangerous the trip could be.

They were thankful for the government snag boats patrolling the river, removing the treacherous trees and other hazards lying just below the water, any of which could pierce the hull of a boat or cause one to become stuck for days.

They passed one steamboat that had been left abandoned by passengers and crew alike when cholera broke out on the boat. Cholera occurred much too often on the river, spreading quickly, and if you were on a crowded boat, you had a much higher chance of coming across someone who was affected by it.

One afternoon, a man was taken into custody and turned over to the local constable at the next landing after he got into a dispute over a card game and shot a man in the arm. The man who had been shot got off as well to receive medical attention. The pistol ball had broken his arm and it might have to be amputated if not treated quickly.

Poker was sometimes frowned upon in some areas or illegal in others and gamblers, mostly cheats, would travel the steamboats where gambling was not only accepted, but gaming tables would be set up in special areas to attract the card players as passengers.

Patrick forbade Mike to play cards or to go to the barroom on the ship. Nothing good would have come from it. The money was not to be thrown away in that manner. They were already gambling on getting to California and finding enough gold to make them rich.

In less than a week, barring any incidents, they would traverse into the Mississippi River, their connection to the Missouri River near St. Louis and the push for Independence, their final steamboat landing. Something Mike would be very happy about. Even Patrick was getting tired of the boat. He escaped into his journal more and more each day.

The pilot came to them a couple days later and told them they were going to be making a landing at Quarantine Island, which was about four miles from St. Louis. It was an ordinance that had to be obeyed by every boat or the captain would be arrested. At Quarantine Island, also known as Arsenal Island, everyone received a medical examination. With over three-hundred people on board, it could take a while.

A cholera outbreak in the city the year before had killed thousands and a fire had destroyed over twenty boats before spreading to the center of the city, burning down fifteen city blocks. 1849 had not been a good year for St. Louis.

Those who were found to be sick or suspected to be ill were removed from the ship and placed in temporary housing on the island. Over fifty people from the ship, mostly those who had stayed on the deck, were kept on the island.

Those not showing any signs of illness were allowed to stay on the ship for a short period and watched for any signs of disease. Once they were cleared, the boat could continue on to St. Louis.

There were many immigrants, mostly German and Irish who became sick while waiting to be checked and died. Those who did were buried on Quarantine Island.

Shortly before arriving at St. Louis, the pilot told them, he was going to have some minor repairs made on the boat that may take an extra day or two longer. It was the only place for them to get the parts they needed. He asked if they wanted to get another boat to Independence, but suggested they may want to stay on board. A cabin might be hard to find on another boat.

The boys agreed that it would be best if they stayed on this boat and continued the trip to Independence after repairs were made. They were warned not to wander far off.

When the boat got to St. Louis, they saw at least a hundred and twenty steamboats at the levee. There were many men working along the levee and there were still boats that had burned in 1849 along the riverfront. It was easy to see where the fire had traveled from the riverfront with many buildings still scorched and other buildings completely burnt to the ground.

St. Louis had been dealt a mighty blow, but it wasn't down for the count. Many buildings were being rebuilt using brick and other fire-resistant materials that a new ordinance called for.

With all the boats coming in, the new railroad, the industry, the push west, St. Louis was going to be just fine and would be a shining city once again, very soon. With over 77,000 inhabitants and the biggest city west of Pittsburgh, it was already well on its way.

CHAPTER 49

Tom Dearing was sitting in the back office of his coin shop. It was well past closing and he just got off the phone with his surveillance team. Warner just left the female detective's apartment. He thought Warner might have stayed longer or maybe even spend the night. Maybe he was wrong about the two of them.

Bill was driving home, but something just wasn't sitting right with him. His keen senses were giving him warning signs. It was nearly midnight and there were not that many cars on the road in that area this time of night.

There was one car that was some ways behind him, keeping its distance no matter how fast or slow he went. It had made the same turns he had, and Bill was now convinced it was following him. Possibly all the way from Vickie's apartment.

That meant someone had followed him there or had been watching Vickie's apartment before he got there. This wasn't good. He opened and reached into his console removing his 9mm S & W semi-auto that was presented to him when he retired. He took it out of the pancake holster returning the holster to the console.

He always had it with him, either on his side or where

he could get to it quickly. He didn't think he would need it in Vickie's apartment, so he left it in his car.

The pistol was fully loaded with one already in the chamber, just as it always was. Not like in the moves or TV where they jacked one in the chamber just before going into action. That was a waste of time and could get you killed.

He flicked off the safety and placed it between his legs, ready for use if the need arose.

Bill didn't want to give the occupant or occupants of the other car any reason to believe he knew he was being followed; not just yet. He continued his path home, keeping his speed regulated and forming a plan.

Bill stopped at a convenience store not too far from his house, watching as the car pulled over almost a half block away and turn its lights off. Before Bill got out, he put the gun inside his waistband in the small of his back, pulling his shirt out to cover it. He got out of his car and went into the store.

Bill went to the clerk, pulled his secondary billfold out and showed him his badge, not bothering to tell him he was retired. He asked about a back door and the clerk showed him the way.

Bill made his way from the back of the store, across a side street, and behind where the other car was located. He knew he would have to hurry, not wanting the person to get too suspicious about how much time he was spending in the store.

Bill was in a vantage spot to see there was only one occupant in the car. If there had been more, he would have called on a patrol car to confront them.

Bill maneuvered to get behind the car, writing down the make, model, color, and license plate before making any move. The driver was fully occupied with the use of binoculars in watching the store, waiting for Bill to come out so the moving surveillance could continue. Bill had other plans.

Bill pulled his pistol and crept along the driver's side of the car, hoping the driver would continue to look through the binoculars and not look in his side mirror.

Bill was going to quickly open the driver's door, he hoped, praying it wasn't locked and surprise the driver. If it was locked, he would bust out the window, and try to keep the driver from driving off, or even worse, shooting him. About now, Bill wished he had called that patrol unit.

Bill grabbed the door handle, took a deep breath and with one quick move, flung the door open, pushing his gun into the driver's terrified face. Bill yelled "Freeze!"

The man dropped the binoculars as he turned and looked Bill in the eyes. His mouth opened like he wanted to say something, but nothing came out. He quickly grabbed the steering wheel with one hand while debating about putting the car in gear with the other.

"If you move, I'll put a bullet in that ugly face of yours

before you can get it in gear," Bill told him, his gun pointed at a spot right in the middle of the man's big unibrow.

The man slowly put his other hand on the steering wheel. "It's not what you think, Detective Warner," the man said, a little shakily.

"I want you to look straight ahead and slowly take the keys out and drop them on the ground," Bill commanded.

The man complied.

"Now I know you have a gun somewhere," Bill stated, "where is it?"

"Shoulder holster, left side," the man replied.

Bill put his gun to the side of the man's head. "Unless you want a bright-red touch-up of your interior, I wouldn't move if I were you," Bill said.

"I'm not moving an inch," the man returned, not even shaking his head as he continued to look forward.

Bill reached into the man's jacket and unfastened the holster, allowing a Colt-1911, .45 cal. to drop into his hand. "Nice," Bill said of the weapon.

"Please, don't drop it on the ground," the man asked. "I have my identification in my right inside jacket pocket."

"And just who do you claim to be?" Bill asked.

"I'm Gerald Olson. I'm a private investigator. I was hired by Mr. Murphy to keep an eye on you and Detective Winston."

"Keep an eye on us? For what reason?" Bill asked

"To make sure you were safe," Olson said.

"Show me your ID," Bill demanded. "Slowly," he added, not moving his gun away.

Olson reached into his jacket pocket and removed a wallet with two fingers, holding it out to Bill.

"Show me," Bill said.

Olson opened the wallet, showing a State of Georgia's private investigator's license issued to Gerald Olson with his picture on it.

"How long have you been watching us?" Bill asked, not so politely.

"Just a couple days," Olson advised. "He was afraid after all the other things going on, someone may try to hurt you or Detective Winston."

"You do understand," Bill began, "that we are both trained law enforcement and are armed all the time?"

"Well, she is anyway," Olson stated. "You're retired."

"So! Whose gun is in whose face?"

"I see your point. Do you mind?"

Bill pointed the gun down but didn't put it away. "So, if you are following me, who's watching Detective Winston?"

"I have a colleague watching her apartment." We weren't supposed to have any contact with you unless it was absolutely necessary.

"Is there anyone else you are keeping an eye on?"

"That's on a need to know basis. You'll have to discuss that with Mr. Murphy."

"He doesn't seem to be around right this minute," Bill said. "I want answers now." He brought the gun back up to point at the man's head.

"Are you really going to kill me? I don't think so." Olson said, a little cocky.

"Are you really going to test me?" Bill asked, now pointing the gun at the man's knee. "You see, I don't have to kill you, I wouldn't get any answers that way. So, I guess I'll just have to show you I'm not to be played with." Bill took deliberate aim at the man knee this time with his finger on the trigger.

"Okay," Olson cried. "You win. He's had my outfit on retainer for some time. We also watch John Gray on a regular basis and do jobs for Mr. Murphy when he needs them done."

"What kind of jobs?" Bill asked.

"The kind you don't tell cops about. That's as far as I'm going with this. If you have to shoot me, go ahead and get it over with, but that's all I'm telling you."

"Call your colleague, have him meet us somewhere close to the apartment. I'll contact Detective Winston and have her join us. I want this all out in the open and then I'll talk to Murphy about this later."

"He may not be too happy about that."

"I don't care," Bill said. "This isn't the way to start out

something and expect people to trust you. It goes both ways."

Olson opened his jacket and slowly removed a phone from its holster on his right side. He pushed a few numbers and waited for an answer. Nothing. The phone continued to ring.

"Okay, so where is this contact?" Bill asked.

"He's supposed to be watching the apartment. If he needed a break or something, he'd call."

"Try again," Bill advised.

Olson tried again; twice, then texted his man. Still nothing.

"Somethings not right," Olson said. "I need to go check on him." He put his hand out like Bill should give him his gun back.

"We'll both go," Bill stated, "I'll hold onto this for just a bit longer." Bill went around and got into the passenger seat.

"Still don't trust me, do you," Olson asked.

"Nope. Don't trust you, don't know you, and sure as heck, not about to put a gun in your hand till I do."

"Fair enough," Olson said, putting the car in gear, heading back towards Vickie's apartment.

Bill had placed the .45 in the small of his back, wanting to be sure of the situation before giving it back, however, he still had a firm hold on his own pistol.

Olson drove with a determined, yet worried look. His man was still not answering.

Bill thought about Vickie. If something happened to the guy watching her apartment, keeping her safe, then what kind of danger could she be in? He got his own phone out and tried to call her. No answer. He tried again. It was possible she may have gone to bed, but then again.

"Step on it!" he told Olson.

Within five minutes, they pulled up to the car Olson's colleague was supposed to be in, a half block from Vickie's apartment. He wasn't there, however, the door was ajar with its window busted in, glass everywhere, and there was blood on the driver's seat and headrest. A set of binoculars was on the passenger seat. The keys were not in the car, yet it was still warm.

"Check around," Olson pleaded, "he's got to be close."

They separated and began checking the area. About fifty feet from the car, Bill came across a set of car keys on the ground. He picked them up and found they were for the same manufacturer as the now abandoned car. Someone had dropped them or thrown them behind the car.

Bill started to ask himself questions when it struck him. He ran back to the car and fit the key into the trunk lock.

Olson, seeing Bill run for the car did so as well. "What did you find?" He asked as the trunk popped open.

Inside the trunk was the missing man, hands and feet bound, his mouth taped. He was unmoving, bloody around the head and shoulders.

Bill reached in, checked for a pulse, and was surprised to find one. "Call 9-1-1," Bill said, "and stay with him, I've got to check on Detective Winston," Bill called out over his shoulder as he started running towards her apartment.

He got to Vickie's door and knocked. The door pushed in just a bit, having not been closed all the way. He still had his gun in his hand and pushed it open a bit more. He didn't see or hear anything. He called out, "Vickie, it's Bill." There was no answer.

He entered the apartment, weapon ready when he saw Vickie come out from a hallway. She wasn't alone. A man stood behind her, shielding himself with her body, gun to her head.

"Drop the gun, cowboy," the man said.

"What do you want?" Bill asked.

"I want you to drop the gun. I won't ask again," he emphasized this by pushing his gun a little harder against Vickie's head, causing it to move forward just a bit.

Bill tossed his gun to the floor, not too far away.

"Nice try, cowboy, now kick it over this way."

Bill kicked his gun several feet towards the guy and Vickie. The man maneuvered Vickie to where the gun was and keeping the gun to her back, reached down and picked it up. He pushed Vickie towards Bill and Bill grabbed her.

"Are you okay?" he asked

"Yeah, just a little headache thanks to the butt of his

gun," she responded. "I've had worse."

"Okay," Bill said to the man who now had two guns pointed at them, "what's this all about?"

"Don't you know?" The man said. "You're stupider than I thought. And they call you Atlanta's Finest. Ha."

"Why don't you give me a clue," Bill challenged him as he guided Vickie behind him, shielding her from the man. Bill put his hands up.

"Isn't that just the gentleman in you," the man sneered, "willing to take the first bullet. But you forget, she gets the second, and from your own gun at that," he tossed his head back some as he let out a big laugh. Just then, the living room light went out.

Bill went down to one knee and there were two quick shots.

The man was propelled backwards into the hallway by the two heavy rounds hitting him in the chest. He fell, dead before he hit the floor just as the light came back on.

Bill turned to Vickie who was still holding the Colt .45 pointed at the man on the floor.

"Nice job," Bill said, maybe a little louder than necessary, the ringing in his ears from the close discharge of the .45 was drowning out every other sound. "How did you make the lights go out just then? It was a good distraction," He turned and went over to the man in the hallway. A quick check confirmed he was dead. Bill retrieved his own gun and took the other from the dead man's hand.

"I didn't," Vickie said, "there's been some strange things going on with the lights lately."

"Good timing whatever it was," Bill said.

"Nice move with the .45 in the small of your back," she said, smiling. "Where'd you get it and speaking of good timing, how did you know I was in trouble?" Vickie asked.

"Looks like I'm collecting them," he said, holding up the dead man's .45 semi-auto. "I'm just glad there was one in the chamber. We both were being watched."

"You mean you didn't know if it was ready to shoot? What if it hadn't?" Vickie asked, looking down at the gun in her hand.

"It's not my gun and anyway, I didn't think there was much of a choice?" Bill said. "Looks like we were being targeted. There's a lot going on and a bunch to tell you."

"Watched? Targeted? I'd love to hear all about it" Vickie stated, "but first, do you mind if we call and get this dead guy out of my apartment?"

William N. Gilmore

CHAPTER 50

St. Louis was one of the many launching and supply points for the overland trail routes, but further up river was Independence and the main trails for the Oregon and the Santa Fe. They were getting close.

There were going to be a lot of boats going to Independence. The river was getting crowded. Already they saw two boats collide, neither wanting to give in to the other, the pilots and crew yelling, cursing at the other, and blowing horns. Luckily, the damage appeared to be minimal.

Patrick and Mike went into the city to check on maps, guidebooks, and supply options. One of the things they wanted to examine was firearms. Neither had much experience but knew it was something they would need, maybe sooner rather than later.

Their first stop was at a gun shop. There was a wide selection of firearms and edged weapons; flintlock muskets and pistols, cap and ball rifles, and revolvers, knives, and swords from all over the world.

Mike really liked the revolvers. He'd never held one and asked if he could. The clerk took it out of the glass case, showed Mike that it was unloaded and handed it to him, grip first.

"This is new. It's an 1848 Colt Dragoon. It's chambered

in .44 caliber and can shoot six times before reloading."

Mike's big hand swallowed up the grip and it felt funny to him.

"So, you've never shot a handgun before?" The clerk asked.

"No," Mike said, "I've never shot anything."

"And what about you, my good man," he asked of Patrick.

"Me? No, I haven't either."

"I bet you're headed to California," the clerk surmised, "you're going to need something for hunting and protection."

"That's what we were thinking," Patrick admitted.

"Well, it seems you may be in need of some lessons too. They're included with the purchase. Would you like to try?" The clerk encouraged.

"What, here?" Mike asked, looking around.

"We have a target site out back if you are interested."

Mike looked at Patrick. Patrick knew the look. "Okay, we'll give it a try."

The clerk took them out the back door where a table was set up. Several yards away was another table with some bottles standing up. A little bit further and to the side was a large plank sticking out of the ground, about as tall as a man. It had some feathers sticking out of the top.

"This is how you load it," the clerk said as he went

through the motions, explaining each step. It took him about two minutes to load the six chambers of the cylinders, pausing at times to make sure the boy's understood how to proceed safely.

After the clerk loaded the pistol, he had Mike stand at the side of the table, with Patrick behind them and handed Mike the big gun.

"Don't point it at anything you don't want to shoot," the clerk emphasized. "Hold your arm out straight and aim it at one of the bottles. Bring the hammer back with your thumb until it clicks twice. Slowly, and I mean slowly, squeeze the trigger as you aim."

"The discharge of the gun startled Mike and Patrick. Mike quickly put the gun back on the table. "Bloody hell!" Mike yelled, hands on both sides of his head. "I've got church bells in me ears."

"Looks like you missed everything, but that's usual for first-timers. Want to try again? Put this cotton in your ears," The clerk offered. "Try the big plank. It's an Indian coming to take your scalp." The clerk said, handing Mike the gun once more. "Take a deep breath and let it out just before you slowly pull the trigger. Don't forget to aim right in the middle. Now pull the hammer back."

The gun wavered in Mike's hand and it seemed to take forever before he did pull the trigger. The loud explosion once again surprised Mike and Patrick, both jumping.

"Well, maybe you scared him to death. Looks like you may need something else." The clerk took the gun and went back inside, returning just a short time later. The clerk now had a double-barreled shotgun with him. He sat down at the table and loaded one barrel. "Let's try this," he said, handing it to Mike. "It's a 12 Gauge. It was made in England."

Mike took aim down the long barrel at the table of bottles, cocked the hammer, and fired. Every bottle broke into pieces, flying off the table. He lowered the shotgun and smiled.

"Now, sir, it's your turn. Shotgun or pistol?" The clerk asked, taking the shotgun from Mike and placing it on the table.

"I want to try the pistol first," Patrick said, giving a wink at Mike.

The clerk went over to a wooden box, got several bottles and took them out to the table, setting them up. He came back to Patrick, removed the pistol from his pocket and had Mike stand behind them.

The clerk handed Patrick the gun, gave him the same advice as he had given Mike and stepped back.

"It's heavier than I thought it would be," Patrick said. He took quick aim, pulled the hammer back and fired. One of the bottles broke in half.

"Nice," the clerk said. "Now try it again. Shoot the green bottle."

Patrick again took a quick aim, firing at the bottle. The

green bottle shattered.

"The clerk looked at Patrick. "Are you sure you've never fired a gun before?"

"I swear that be the truth," Patrick said.

"Okay, there's two shots left," the clerk said, "try hitting the Indian both times."

Patrick raised the gun, cocked the hammer, fired, cocked the hammer quickly and fired again, all like it was in one motion.

The clerk smiled, knowing Patrick had to have missed. He took the gun from Patrick and they began to walk towards the plank. As they got closer through the blue smoke, the clerk's mouth opened. He saw it from a distance. There, centered just a few inches below the feathers were two round holes. Kill shots.

Mike looked at Patrick. "You get to protect us if Indians attack," Mike said, "I'll kill all the bottles."

"We'll take them both," Patrick said, "plus balls, caps, and powder for each. Is there anything else we'll need?"

"There are cleaning kits that come with them. I might suggest a holster for the Colt," the clerk offered, "It would be easier to carry. For the shotgun, you'll be wanting a selection of shot. Everything from birdshot to balls for big game."

"Okay," Patrick replied, "if you'll be kind enough to pack up a four-month supply, we'll be back later to get them."

"Would you care to leave a deposit, sir? It will hold the guns and supplies for you."

"I think you should hold the guns for us," Mike said, giving the clerk a stern look. "We will be back."

"Yes, sir," the clerk answered, not wanting to make the big man mad, "it won't be a problem. I'll clean the guns myself, have everything packed up, and have your bill ready when you return. Thank you, gentlemen."

The boys left the gun shop and only had to go a few stores down to find a general mercantile where they could get the guidebooks they were seeking.

There was a book for Mormons going to Oregon, books on gold prospecting, a book about Indians, and a book on the Santa Fe trail. There was even a list of supplies suggested.

"You may want to get your supplies here," the store clerk suggested, "the price is only going to get higher up river. We've got the best prices in St. Louis, guaranteed."

"We're not set up yet," Mike said, "we don't even have a wagon yet."

"Well, we can get that taken care of right here," The clerk said smiling "if you have the money, that is."

Patrick quickly stepped in. "We're working on that. Maybe we'll come back when we have the funds."

"You do that," the clerk said with a huff, turned and with his nose in the air, went to help someone else.

"Patrick turned to Mike and said, "We don't want people knowing we have money. Not before we get those guns."

CHAPTER 51

Blue and red lights gave the scene an almost psychedelic effect as Vickie sat at the back of an ambulance having her head looked at by an EMT. She jerked when he applied the hydrogen peroxide. Not so much from the sting as from how cold it was.

"Hold this to your head for at least five minutes," the EMT said, taking her hand and placing it on the bandage. "You'll live. There's not enough peroxide in the world for the guy inside though" he said laughing and held his gloved hand up for Bill to tap. "Good shooting."

"Thanks," Bill said, ignoring the hand. "Your patient here did that and I would suggest you not piss her off."

"Well, I, ah—er, sorry about that, Detective," he directed at Vickie. "Umm, if there's anything else you need, you let us know." He took off quickly for the front of the ambulance.

Lt. Cummings of the Homicide Squad walked up to the two, shaking his head. "Busy night around here," he said. "This have anything to do with the PI that got roughed up and stuffed in the trunk of a car just down the road?"

"Yeah, just a little bit," Bill said. He pulled the Colt out from behind him. "This belongs to his boss. It's the gun Vickie used to shoot the guy in the apartment, I took it from him earlier" tonight, when I found out he was following me."

The lieutenant's mouth hung open for a few seconds "Would you mind starting from the beginning. Slowly."

Bill gave him the information on what had transpired, leaving out a few things like the dinner, Mr. Murphy, the partnership, treasure, and Vickie thinking about retiring."

"It sounds like a good shooting, but I can see there are a few holes that need to be filled in. Anything you want to share now while it's fresh?"

"No, I think that's about it," Bill said. Vickie was shaking her head. "Have you identified the body?"

"Not yet, but I'm sure it won't be long. Someone like that is bound to be in the system."

Gerald Olson walked over to the ambulance. "Are you okay, Detective Winston?"

"Yes, I'll be fine, thank you."

"How's your man?" Bill asked.

"He may have a concussion and a broken nose, but he'll be alright."

"That's good," Bill said. "It could have been worse."

"Yeah. May I get my gun back now, Mr. Warner?"

"Lieutenant, this is Gerald Olson," Bill introduced the man. "He's one of the PI's who was watching us. Sorry, Gerald, it's going to have to be turned in as evidence."

"Evidence? I told you everything. I have a license for it."

"Yeah, about that, we'll talk later, but we used your gun on the guy who took out your guy. He was trying to kill Vickie and me. He didn't make it."

"You killed someone with *my* gun?"

"Well, technically no. It was her," Bill said, thumbing over at Vickie. "She was doing your job."

"But I —" Olsen started.

"I need to have a few words with you, Mr. Olson, if you don't mind," Lt. Cummings said. "Come over here to my car," taking Olson by the arm and began to walk him away from the ambulance "You have the right to remain silent…"

"You're not staying here tonight," Bill said. "You're coming home with me."

"I am?" Vickie said. "This was awfully quick. After only one dinner and saving your life and all. You move fast."

"You know what I mean," Bill said. "For one thing, I'm not sure you are safe here and then there is a mess to clean up. I'll help you with that latter, but for now, you can come and stay in my guest room for as long as you want."

"Didn't you say you had a burglary there? Safe? I don't know."

"I put in a new security system and—

"I'm just kidding, thanks, I'd like that. I wouldn't want to stay here tonight anyway. It's all going to be marked as a crime scene and I'd never get any rest."

"You're sure your head is okay?" Bill asked. "No concussion, blurred vision, or anything?"

"I'm good. I can even drive. In fact, I want to," Vickie insisted," I don't want to leave my car here or have to rely on you for my transportation."

"I don't mind, but if that's what you want. I'll go check with Lieutenant Cummings and see if we can go. We can make our written statements tomorrow. I might even give Olsen a little help. I think he's okay."

"I'll go grab a few things if they'll let me. Shouldn't be but just a few minutes, partner."

Bill smiled.

Vickie went to her apartment and checked with the CSI supervisor about getting some things from her bedroom. The body had already been removed, however, there was a large blood splatter on the wall and blood stains on the carpet in the hallway, and small numbered markers spread around.

She went into the bedroom and went to the closet for a small suitcase. She opened the door and reached in for the case. She noticed that some of her clothes had been rearranged. Some of the clothes on hangers had been pushed to one side and others pushed to the other. There was one item sitting in the middle. She picked up the hanger and found it to be a dress she had never worn. One she had bought for a special occasion that never came. She had thought about wearing it tonight but decided it wasn't time.

Someone from the CSI team must have been looking in the closet, she thought. She put the suitcase on her bed and opened it, placing items she thought she may need including items from her bathroom for a day or two stay. She turned and looked at the closet, walked over and grabbed the dress, folding it carefully and placing it into the case.

She walked out of her room and saw the CSI supervisor. "What were you all looking for in my closet?" She asked.

"We didn't look in your closet, Detective. Is there a problem?"

"No, never mind, my mistake," Vickie said. She walked back out to her car and put the suitcase in. Then she found Bill who got permission from the lieutenant for them to leave if they promised to make their statements sometime the next day.

"You lead the way, I'll follow," Vickie stated.

"Then we're off," Bill said.

"Yes," Vickie agreed, "we must be."

Bill nodded his head and laughed.

Arriving at Bill's house, automatic lights came on as they parked side by side. Bill helped Vickie with her bag and got the front door unlocked. Once in, he turned the alarm off.

"Oh, Bill, it's lovely," Vickie said, looking around.

"A lot of it was my wife's decorating. I haven't changed too much."

"Come on in and make yourself at home. I'll give you the five-cent tour.

Bill took her around the house, ending at the guest room where he put her suitcase by the bed. If you need or want anything, don't ask, just get it. I know it's late, but when you are settled in, come out to the dining room, I have something to show you."

"Okay, I'll be there in just a minute. Thanks again. This is nice."

"No. Thank you. Without you, I wouldn't be coming home ever again."

"Don't forget Mr. Olson."

"Right. I told the lieutenant he was straight and to give him a break. They sent him on his way for now. Guess he'll need to make a statement too."

Bill was sitting at the dining room table when Vickie came in and sat down with him.

"Coffee or a soft drink? A hard drink?" Bill asked.

"No thanks, I'm still a little wound up. Hope I can sleep a bit. What did you want to show me?"

Bill reached inside his jacket and brought out a billfold. "I found it on the dead guy. It's got his ID and stuff in it."

"Bill, you should have given that to the lieutenant."

"I would have if it were some other case, but this is the guy who tried to kill us. I want to know and I'm not sure if the lieutenant would have given us the information straight away. I mean if you have a problem with it, I'll give it back to the lieutenant and say we found it outside."

Vickie shook her head. "No, I want to know too, who is he?" Vickie asked.

"I don't know, I haven't looked yet."

"Well?" Vickie said, "What are you waiting for, an engraved invitation?"

Bill opened the billfold and saw a driver's license with a picture of the dead guy. He took it out and looked closer at it. "Oops," Bill said. "This might have just gotten a little stickier."

"Why, who is he?" Vickie asked.

"Adam Dearing," Bill said. "Unless there is a big coincidence, I believe he is related to that crooked coin dealer Sam and I went to. They could be brothers."

"You believe he's behind this, whatever this is? Why would he want us dead?"

"I don't know. It must be connected to Murphy somehow and possibly the treasure. How he knows about it, I don't know that either. He began going through the billfold again. There were several business cards, including one for the coin shop. He showed it to Vickie. "I knew it," he said, disgusted. There was also a card for John Gray's dive shop. "I sure hope he's not involved with these guys."

"Me too," Vickie said, "he seemed so nice."

"Murphy trusts him, knew his father too. We'll see."

"Do you think we should tell Mr. Murphy?" Vickie asked.

"Not yet, we'll play it by ear and see where it goes, but we'll need to find out soon. Our list of people to trust isn't getting any bigger."

"It's best if we don't trust anyone, yet"

"Well, I know I trust you."

"Same goes here." She yawned. "Excuse me, guess I'm more whipped than I thought."

"Okay then, time for us to go to bed," Bill said.

Vickie cocked her head, looking at Bill.

"I mean, time to get some sleep," he corrected. "there's a lot going on tomorrow."

Vickie smiled as she got up. "Sleep tight, and don't forget I'm here. I don't want you to shoot me in the dark."

"Oh, I won't forget," he said. "Goodnight."

CHAPTER 52

Patrick and Mike decided to look around a bit, before buying anything else. They found a bank, the Boatmen's Bank, and decided to check their offer for exchange of some of the gold sovereigns. They were able to make a trade and had more of the U. S. silver and gold coins to use. This way, they knew they were not being swindled when making purchases.

There was a horse-drawn omnibus, gas street lights, police officers, beautiful parks, magnificent buildings the fire had not touched, telegraph poles and lines, and many modern things at which the boys gawked.

They came across a much larger mercantile than the first one they had gone into. When they entered, they were immediately approached by a gentleman, dressed in a fancy suit.

"How may I serve you?" he asked.

"We're just here to see what you've got," Patrick said, expecting the man to quickly turn and walk away with his nose in the air.

"Very good, sir," he said, "if you need any assistance, please let me know, my name is Robert. I am proud to say we have the biggest inventory and the very best prices in town."

"Yeah, we've heard that one before," Mike said.

"Well, this time, it's true. Look for yourselves."

"We don't have much money," Patrick advised, testing the helpful clerk.

"That's fine," he said, "you go ahead and look around, enjoy yourself, and if you find something you need, maybe we can work something out. Just let me know."

"Okay, we will," Patrick stated. "Thanks."

"Yeah, thanks," Mike repeated.

They looked around and saw all kinds of items; everything from fancy clothes for dudes to canned food; tools and hardware, boots and hats, even furniture, kitchen supplies, and mining equipment. They even saw the information guides they saw at the other store and sure enough, they were cheaper.

"Maybe we should go ahead and buy what we need here," Mike said.

"We won't have room in the cabin," Patrick said, "besides, we don't want someone to get sticky fingers while we might be out. It would just invite someone to try and take what we have."

"Not if we have those guns, they won't," Mike stated.

"Let's not chance it just yet. If the ship has a problem or there's a sickness, we could lose everything before we even get to Independence."

"I see your point. That's smart thinking," Mike returned, "but I'm glad we're getting the guns."

"Me too," Patrick said. "I hope I never have to use it though."

"Same here," Mike said, "I'd go bloody deaf."

The boys met back up with Robert requesting to buy some of the books on routes and information for their trip overland. Something to read while still on the boat.

On a whim, Mike asked Robert about the hats and he was happy to show him the selection. He tried on several, some looking ridiculous and some looking too elegant; each one with some snide comment from Patrick. He tried on a big brimmed, tan felt hat that fit him well. After some discussion, Mike got Patrick to consider buying him the hat, thinking it would make him look more American and even more imposing than he already did.

"It's a fine choice," Robert stated. "This would keep the sun and the rain off you and it's one of our most popular sellers. You can mold the crown as well to make it your very own and tighten the hatband to make it fit just the way you want. And you sir," he said, turning to Patrick, "you might find the protection useful as well. Would you like to try one on?"

"No thanks," Patrick returned. "At two dollars apiece, we could go broke mighty quick buying junk like that."

"You want me to die of heatstroke?" Mike asked. "Or get rain down my back and catch my death of cold?"

Patrick took in a deep breath, letting it out long and loud

before he responded. "I'll buy the bloody hat for you, but I'm keeping a tally of what you will owe me later. If you lose it or it gets swept away in the wind, you are out of luck."

"Don't you think you should get one too?" Mike questioned. "You'll burn the top of your head."

"Not now," Patrick insisted. "Maybe in Independence."

They went to the front of the store where Patrick paid for the books and the hat. They thanked Robert and headed out. Once outside, Patrick handed Mike the wrapped bundle that contained his hat. Mike tore open the paper and put the hat on proudly, giving it a slight cock to fit his big head.

"Well, what do you think?" Mike asked.

"I think you owe me two more dollars."

"No, really, what do you think?"

"Tilt it down just a little," Patrick said.

Mike did.

"A little more."

Mike tilted the front brim again. Now, the hat covered most of Mike's face.

"Now, you look like a bloody American."

Mike quickly pushed the hat back on his head. "You were joshing me, weren't you?"

"Let's go pick up the guns and supplies and head back to the boat," Patrick suggested. "We'll come back out tomorrow. It's still going to be a day or two before it leaves."

CHAPTER 53

Bill got out of the shower and smelled the bacon. Vickie must have gotten up earlier and started breakfast. He smiled.

He shaved and dressed, making his way out to the kitchen expecting to see Vickie at the stove or at the table.

"Good morning, Dad," Jenny said.

"Hi, Grandpa. Mom's cooking us some breakfast."

"Retirement letting you sleep later than usual, I see," his daughter stated. "Whose car is that out in the driveway?"

Bill stood there, looked at Sam and tried to come up with an appropriate answer.

"It's mine," Vickie said, coming into the kitchen.

"Oh, I'm sorry," Jenny said, herself now looking at Sam. "I didn't know you had—company."

"Your father let me use the guest room for a couple days," Vickie said. "My apartment is getting cleaned. I'm Vickie Winston."

"She's an old friend from the police department," Bill said quickly.

"I remember," Jenny said, "It's been a while though."

"Hi, Detective," Sam said, with a big smile. "It's good to see you again. Are you hungry?"

"Yes, as a matter of fact, I am," she said.

Jenny gave her father a funny look and smiled. "Everyone have a seat. How do you like your eggs, Ms. Winston? Or should I say, Detective?"

"It's Vickie, and any old way is fine with me, thanks."

"Are you going to be protecting Caution and her mother now?" Sam asked.

"I'm still trying to decide," Vickie said. "There's a lot to consider. Your grandpa has been helping me."

"I like her and her dad, she's got a nice dog too," Sam said.

Jenny turned to her father. "I figure you were about to catch me up on just what you and Sam have been up to lately," Jenny said, narrowing her eyes. "Is there something you wanted to share?"

"Maybe in a little while, breakfast smells so good, I'm getting really hungry, is there any toast?" Bill unsuccessfully tried to change the subject.

"Who or what is Caution?" Jenny continued.

"She's neat, Mom. She lives in this huge house and she's rich."

"Sam, we'll get into all this later, right now, let's enjoy a good breakfast. Vickie and I have to go by the police department and then check on her apartment. It's going to be a busy day."

"Can I come too?" Sam asked, excited about the

prospects of going to the police department. "Can I, Mom?"

"I'm sorry, but not today, Sam," his grandfather said. "I have too much to do and I won't be able to spend any real time with you, but next time, we'll have all day together."

"Shucks," Sam said, disappointed. "Okay."

"Besides," Jenny started, "We had plans to get you a haircut and do some shopping."

"You help your mom out today," Grandpa Bill said, "and we'll plan something real soon, okay partner?" He gave Sam a wink.

Sam understood and gave a wink back. "Okay, partner."

Jenny put out a large plate of scrambled eggs and another plate of bacon. She put a smaller plate of several slices of toast down on the table. Bill looked up and smiled. She didn't.

She sat at the table and everyone took hands as she gave thanks for the food, safety, and well-being for everyone, and guidance for herself.

After breakfast, Bill and Vickie left for the police department. They took his car.

"I knew exactly what she was thinking when I came out," Vickie said, breaking a long silence. "I don't blame her. I'd think the same. I hope I didn't embarrass you."

"I wasn't embarrassed I was just surprised. I didn't know they were coming over. I hope I didn't put you in an embarrassing position."

"We have nothing to be embarrassed about," Vickie said. "Even if we were together, we're adults and don't have to explain things to anyone."

"Not to Sam, of course, he's too young to really understand. I think it just surprised my daughter some to think that we were. There hasn't been anyone else since—well, you know."

"Same here," Vickie nodded. "You haven't told your daughter anything about Mr. Murphy?"

"Not yet. Nothing about the coin, our meeting, or anything that has been going on. I was going to, but with everything last night, I'm not sure now if I should."

"You don't think Sam is in any danger, do you?" Vickie asked, concerned.

"I doubt it. If I really did think he was, things would be different."

"How?"

"If I thought there was a real danger to Sam, and I knew who that threat was, there might be more bodies popping up."

"I can't say I'd blame you," Vickie said.

CHAPTER 54

The boys returned to the gun shop for the guns and the other supplies. The entire cost was almost fifty dollars which Mike thought was rather high. They returned to the boat and had to store the gunpowder in a cool, dry place, so Patrick wrapped the two small kegs in a blanket and put them in a corner, away from any lantern.

It took two days for the repairs to be completed on the boat. In the meantime, Patrick and Mike took turns reading the books with the information about the trails to California as well as how to pan and mine for gold.

They had gone out only once more and ate at one of the fancy restaurants, both having large steaks that covered the entire plate; a St. Louis special.

Once they were back on the river, their excitement about getting to Independence, and on the trail, had risen considerably. The almost two weeks it took to get there were filled with non-stop talks and plans.

Using one of the books they bought, an 1849 guide made by Joseph Ware listing the suggested amounts of food items they would need per person, they made a list and as the trip wore on, they kept updating the list. The rest of the trip included cleaning their weapons and re-reading the books.

They believed they were well prepared for the overland part of their trip. Maybe they were better prepared than most, however, they really had no idea what was to come. The boys were soon about to become men.

Independence had many more boats than Pittsburgh but maybe not as many as St. Louis. The wharf was busy with boats unloading and loading; wagons, supplies, cattle, horses, even oxen, and mules. People were everywhere; workers, families, and travelers from all over. Sometimes they saw two or more people yelling at each other in different languages which neither Patrick nor Mike had ever heard.

One of their first objectives was to find a wagon train leaving soon for California along the California trail and get signed up with the wagon master. After that, they decided they should get a hotel room until the wagon train leaves, get a wagon, the supplies required, and all the items on their list.

It wasn't long before they found that things had changed considerably over the past few months. There were still many wagon trains leaving from Independence, however, due to the cholera epidemic that had spread with the westward movement of sick immigrants to Independence, many of the wagon trains that had left from the city center were now getting their start a little further north in places like St. Joseph, Weston, or Council Bluffs.

Flat-bottomed barges could be hired to transport wagons, animals, and supplies to these other jump-off cities. Some even kept the wagons from having to cross rivers, which was always a tricky maneuver.

It was now nearing the end of May and time was beginning to grow short to start out on the routes west. The wagons had to wait for the rains of early spring to pass as well as the grass on the prairie to grow to feed the animals along the way. Leaving too late might find them without water or food, or possibly stranded in snow in the high passes like the unfortunate Donner-Reed party did just a few years back.

The Donner party having traveled from Springfield, Illinois to Independence, arrived there in May 1846. The day after their arrival, they pushed on for California. Along the way, they encountered many problems that delayed them, including the illness and eventual death of one of its members, Indians killing many of their animals, and deciding to use the untested shortcut of the Hastings Pass, even after being warned not to take that route.

The Pass was found to be nearly unusable, too rocky for the wagons and unsure footing for walking, causing damage to the wagons and injuries to those on foot, including the animals.

Early snows blocked the pass that caused them to become stranded for the winter in the Sierra Mountains. Of the eighty-seven people who had once made up the group, including many women and children, nearly half didn't survive.

There were terrible rumors about what some of the members of the party had done in order to survive.

The boys learned of several parties leaving from St. Joseph in the next week or so. They also found a wagon maker there in Independence who had wagons already constructed and ready for sale.

Hiram Young, a former slave, had recently come to Independence and opened a business making freight wagons and oxen yokes. Working for him were both freedman, white men and also slaves, who could earn their freedom.

Young was believed to have paid first for his wife, Matilda's freedom and then his own by carving yoke for oxen. Most of his business was through a government contract, but he also built wagons for those who wanted to go west. His wagons were said to be some of the best constructed wagons for the rugged travel.

Patrick and Mike purchased a Hiram Young wagon, one that was about half the size of one of the government freight wagons. Besides being of excellent quality, you could identify one of his wagons with the Hiram Young initials branded on its sides. Also, they bought six of the yokes and all the chains, wheel grease, harnesses, and riggings they would need for the trip.

Hiram directed them to where they could buy oxen for

pulling the wagon. Oxen were cheaper than horses or mules and could handle the trip much better. They were slower; however, they were stronger, needed less food and water, and if needed, they could be used as food.

The captains or wagon masters insisted that there be minimum provisions per person for the 2,000-mile trips, which would take between four to six months, besides other recommendations before parties were allowed to join.

Buffalo, deer, fish, bear, elk, and other game could still be found along most trails but could not always be depended on. Many took extra horses, mules, or oxen as well as cattle, calves, and sheep along as either a food source or a starter herd for the future homesteads, if they survived the trip, didn't wander off, or get stolen by Indians.

Cooking on the trail where a fuel source was hard to find had the travelers relying on dried buffalo chips; easy to burn, with no odor, and not much smoke. They were easy to find and pick up. It was a good chore for children walking along the trail.

Almost everyone walked. The only people who rode in the wagons were the injured or ill, babies, or pregnant women who were too far along to be able to walk.

The wagons were kept as light as possible to keep the animals from working too hard. Many coveted items ended up being discarded along the way because of their excess weight. Stoves, beds, tools, musical instruments, barrels, and other items would be left on the side of the trail.

With all the traveling, the wagon and animals, supplies, and weapons, Patrick and Mike had spent nearly a third of the money. They shouldn't need much on the trail except to resupply from one of the forts or sutlers along the way.

They planned to travel as light as possible. They were lucky not to have families to worry about, but they knew the trip would be rough enough for just the two of them. They had bought a horse with saddle and riding equipment as well as doubling-up on some of the food and other essentials, deciding to wait till they got to California to buy all the equipment they would need for finding gold. It would be much more expensive, but even more so if it had to be left behind or lost along the way.

The main load other than the tools, supplies, and food and water was the big chest that Patrick insisted come along. Besides being useful, it was like a good luck piece. It went where he did. It would hold the clothes, extra boots and shoes, blankets, and other essentials needed to be kept dry.

Patrick and Mike would travel with a group leaving out of St. Joseph and might later combine with another group from Independence along the Oregon Trail. Groups traveling from Council Bluffs and other locations might be met and would travel along the same trails until they needed to split up for other destinations.

The young partners were now on their way to California.

CHAPTER 55

Before arriving at police headquarters, Bill and Vickie went to Vickie's apartment. The door was locked, and yellow crime scene tape made a crisscross over the entrance. A patrol unit had been left for security.

They checked with the officer and then made entry to Vickie's apartment. It had a smell to it; blood, gunpowder, death.

"You might want to grab a few more things for a longer stay at my place if you'd like. This may take a while to clean up and air out."

"I'm not sure I want to come back here," Vickie stated, wrinkling her nose.

"I don't blame you," Bill returned, also disgusted with the foul odors. "You can stay at my place till you find a new location."

"I don't think I'll get my cleaning deposit back," she said. "No big loss, considering." She packed another suitcase and a tote with items from the fridge. "No need for the food to go bad, I'll cook for us tonight if you'd like?"

"If it's anything like last night," he said, "I'll just hire you as my full-time cook."

"You can't afford me," she laughed.

"Then maybe I should just—" Bill stopped before he finished.

"You should just, what?" Vickie asked, laughing.

Bill had turned red, was stammering, and fighting to come up with an appropriate answer other than the one that was sitting in the back of his brain and had almost come out his now dry mouth.

"You were saying?" she asked, head cocked to the side.

"That I should buy a fast food franchise," Bill lied.

"Yeah, right. Like all that fast food is good for you. All that grease and salt, you'd be a walking heart attack. You'd need to keep a cardiologist on retainer."

As they left, locking the door behind them, Bill stopped again at the officer's cruiser. He handed him the billfold that came from Adam Dearing. "I found this in the apartment, you may want to get it to the lead detective as evidence." It wasn't a lie, it just wasn't time sensitive.

Bill and Vickie left en route to police headquarters once again. Along the way, they discussed what they should say in their statements. No lies, of course, but all the information did not have to be disclosed right then.

A lot had occurred in a short time and Bill tried to wrap his head around it.

Bill was convinced that the burglary at the Murphy's home and his own were related. He also believed that the assault on Mr. Murphy, and now, the one on Vickie, were related as well, but to find out that Dearing was involved, convinced him that there was a conspiracy, conceivably involving the coins, a possible treasure, and now, the partnership.

Bill still had many questions, not the least of which was how Dearing came to know about the treasure, and how much he knows. How did two, non-existent British coins come to show up on the East Coast; and why did Mr. Murphy want to establish a partnership. There were so many more questions and very few answers.

*

Caution and Molly were out in the back of the estate while her mother was in the kitchen and her father was just leaving his office for the day.

The buzzer for the gated driveway sounded and Mrs. Murphy answered. A man said he had a large package for delivery to a Mr. Murphy. She buzzed him in.

Soon, the doorbell rang, and Mrs. Murphy went to the door. At first, she had a problem unlocking the door and then the door appeared to be stuck as if something was pushing against it. She finally was able to tug the door open.

When it did open, two men in blue jumpsuits, one with a clipboard and the other with a two-wheeled cart carrying a large box about the size of a clothes dryer, asked if she were Mrs. Murphy. She politely stated she was and he asked her to sign some papers to show delivery had been made.

She asked what the item was, and the man stated he did not know, he was just the delivery man.

As she took the clipboard, they pushed their way in and one man grabbed her, putting a cloth over her nose and mouth as the other closed the door. She struggled with them, attempting to yell out, but within just a few seconds, Mrs. Murphy stopped struggling and went limp in the man's hold.

Mr. Murphy arrived home sometime later, calling out to his wife and Caution. There was no answer which was not unusual. He smelled food cooking and strolled into the kitchen only to find a pot roast cooking in the oven. He smiled.

Once again, he called out, but again there was no answer. He started to look around, calling out as he checked every room downstairs. Finally, he went upstairs to their bedroom and upon opening the door, he found his wife on the bed, hands and feet bound, tape over her mouth and eyes. She wasn't moving.

He quickly checked her and found she was breathing yet unresponsive. He removed the tape from her face, hands, and feet. He yelled out for Caution as he ran to her bedroom, checking every area including the balcony, but she wasn't there. He yelled several times, running to each room, but coming up empty. Even Molly was not there.

He ran back to their bedroom and dialed 9-1-1 asking for an ambulance and the police. With them on the way, he checked on his wife once more. She was starting to come around, moaning.

He hated to leave her, but he had to find Caution. He ran downstairs, calling, screaming her name. There was no answer.

He ran to the door leading to the backyard and went out calling for her. He didn't get a response, but he saw something black and white off in the tall grass. It was Molly. She had been hurt and wasn't moving. There was blood around her mouth and on her coat. Caution was not with her. He gently picked Molly up and carried her into the house, placing her on a sofa. The dog was alive but unconscious.

Soon, the police arrived and shortly after, an ambulance. Mrs. Murphy was now conscious and being treated. It appeared she had been knocked out with some chemical such as chloroform or ether. She refused to be transported to the hospital until Caution was found. She gave the police all the information she could recall about the two men.

Molly was carefully placed into one of the police cars and taken to an area vet by one of the officers.

Mr. Murphy and the police continued to search for Caution in the house and on the grounds, but she was nowhere to be found. An officer found a place not far from where Molly was located where the grass had been flattened. He observed and noted there was a cloth with a chemical smell. Blood was also observed in the grassy area. A blood trail led back to the house and around to the main driveway.

Everything was cordoned off with yellow crime scene tape and a Crime Scene Investigation Unit began to search for and gather evidence.

Mr. Murphy rejoined his wife who had mostly recovered from the effects of the unknown chemical agent and was giving a statement to the detectives.

The FBI was notified and soon, several of the agents from the Atlanta Field Office arrived including a recent addition to the office, Special Agent Tommy McGill. The FBI and the Atlanta Police Department would work jointly on the case.

Mr. Murphy called Detective Winston who was still at the Police Headquarters with Bill and gave her the information about Caution and asked for her help. Together, Vickie and Bill rushed to the Murphy estate.

The FBI set up recording devices for the telephones in the Murphy home in case kidnappers called with demands. Local cameras were being checked for any suspicious vehicles, including delivery vans and trucks. Mrs. Murphy had mentioned that she thinks she saw a white delivery style van in the driveway while the men were at the door just before the attack on her.

She couldn't give much of a description of the men because they were wearing hats with the brims pulled down and both were wearing the same style blue jumpsuits. She believed that one of the men may have had a large, dark mustache, but she could not remember which one.

With Caution missing, she was distraught and had trouble focusing on anything else right then. Maybe in a while when there was some word and she was fully recovered she could give more information.

Special Agent Tommy McGill knew that time was a major factor right then and every minute counted. The information they had so far would have to do until Mrs. Murphy was, if possible, able to fill in more.

One of the officers went over to Agent McGill and spoke privately with him for a few minutes.

"Mr. and Mrs. Murphy," Agent McGill began in his thick Irish tongue, "I have good news about your dog."

"Oh, yes, Molly," Mr. Murphy said. "How is she?"

"What happened to Molly, Sean?" Mrs. Murphy asked.

He gave her a quick update on finding her out back.

"The officer who took your dog—Molly, to the vet's office radioed in. Molly is now conscious, but she apparently suffered a concussion from being hit or kicked in the head. She should recover, but she's going to be kept overnight for observation."

"That's good news," Mr. Murphy said.

"Molly means the world to Caution and I feel it's the same with Molly." Mrs. Murphy said.

What Special Agent McGill didn't tell the Murphy's is

that the officer also reported that the blood found on Molly didn't come from her. The blood belonged to a human.

Vickie and Bill arrived at the Murphy's and as soon as Mrs. Murphy saw her, she ran to embrace her.

"Find her, please find her," Mrs. Murphy sobbed.

I hope you have enjoyed reading *Caution in the Wind: Partnerships* and will continue to follow the adventures of Caution, her Great-Great-Grandpa Patrick and his partner Mike, as well as Bill, his Grandson Sam, and their friend Vicky. And don't forget about Molly and all the other exciting characters, good and bad.

The adventures will continue in *Caution in the Wind: The Treasure Seekers,* where Patrick and Mike make the hard and dangerous journey across the new frontier trails to the California gold fields in the hopes of striking it rich. The boys meet characters right out of history and travel to locations before they became famous.

A dark faction uses desperate measures to try to force the Murphy's into revealing the location of a historic treasure, possibly, worth countless millions of dollars. One that may have changed the face of the nation, if not the world.

And a priceless, little girl, with a very canny ability, knows that real treasure lies in the love of family and friends.

You don't want to stop now. You've already become part of this adventure and have met some interesting characters and have witnessed some history as it happened. Come see it through. There's no telling where it may take you and who you might encounter. It could even reveal some of your own history.

Thank you,

William N. Gilmore

Caution in the Wind
Book Two: The Treasure Seekers
Coming Soon